Go for goal with these exciting and action-packed soccer stories!

Take a grandstand seat for some great football action: a barefoot boy who beats the odds and amazes everyone with his stunning skills; a goalie called Titch, who proves height isn't everything when it comes to saving goals; and the one and only Harry Jackson, determined to be the best referee ever.

Kick off your reading now and you'll catch football fever!

www.booksattransworld.co.uk/childrens

Also available by Tony Bradman,
and published by Doubleday/Corgi Books:

GOOD SPORTS! A BAG OF SPORTS
STORIES

AMAZING ADVENTURE STORIES

FANTASTIC SPACE STORIES

INCREDIBLE CREEPY STORIESw

SENSATIONAL CYBER STORIES

GRIPPING WAR STORIES

FOOTBALL FEVER 2

FOOTBALL FEVER

COLLECTED BY
TONY BRADMAN

ILLUSTRATED BY JON RILEY

CORGI BOOKS

FOOTBALL FEVER
A CORGI BOOK : 0 552 52974 5

First publication in Great Britain

PRINTING HISTORY
Corgi edition published 1998

5 7 9 10 8 6

Collection copyright © 1998 by Tony Bradman
Back to Front copyright © 1998 by Rob Childs
The Black Pearl copyright © 1998 by Jonathan Kebbe
Banana copyright © 1998 by Neil Arksey
Up the Pinks! copyright © 1998 by Emily Smith
As Long As It Takes copyright © 1998 by Dennis Hamley
There's Only One Harry Jackson copyright © 1998 by Dennis Hamley
Star on a Desert Island copyright © 1998 by Brian Morse
Daniel Saves the Day? copyright © 1998 by Elizabeth Dale
The Mouth copyright © 1998 by Nick Warburton
Go! Go! Chichico! copyright © 1998 by Geraldine McCaughrean

Illustrations copyright © 1998 by Jon Riley

The right of Tony Bradman to be identified as the author
of this work has been asserted in accordance with
the Copyright Designs and Patents Act 1988.

Condition of Sale
This book is sold subject to the condition that it shall not, by way of trade or
otherwise, be lent, re-sold, hired out or otherwise circulated without the
publisher's prior consent in any form of binding or cover other than that in
which it is published and without a similar condition including this condition
being imposed on the subsequent purchaser.

Set in Bembo by Falcon Oast Graphic Art

Corgi Books are published by Transworld Publishers,
61–63 Uxbridge Road, London W5 5SA,
a division of The Random House Group Ltd,
in Australia by Random House Australia (Pty) Ltd,
20 Alfred Street, Milsons Point, Sydney, NSW 2061, Australia,
in New Zealand by Random House New Zealand Ltd,
18 Poland Road, Glenfield, Auckland 10, New Zealand
and in South Africa by Random House (Pty) Ltd,
Endulini, 5A Jubilee Road, Parktown 2193, South Africa

Printed and bound in Great Britain by
Cox & Wyman Ltd, Reading, Berkshire.

CONTENTS

BACK TO FRONT
by Rob Childs

'Open goal!'

'I don't believe it! How did he miss that?'

'C'mon, wake your ideas up!'

You just ought to have heard 'em. But I suppose if you're a footballer like me, you already know what I'm talking about – the sound of parents doing their nut on the touchline. I tried to ignore it all, but it's not easy when you're being laughed at, is it? Especially when you're the school team's leading scorer.

'Forget it, Everton,' our captain said. 'Can't score every time.'

'Soz,' I sighed, giving him a kind of daft, lopsided grin to try and cover my embarrassment. 'Just one of those days, like, I guess.'

Typical! It was meant to be a dead special day, an' all.

1

I wanted everything to go just right, but the morning had gone and started off all wrong. We were losing 1–0 and messing up so many chances, it looked like we'd never score.

Got to admit that last one *was* a sitter. It just came to me a bit sudden and I stubbed my toe on the ground as I shot. Total miskick, it was, and the ball wobbled past the post like a drunk.

Might have been different, if I could have headed it! Most of my goals are headers. I'm big for my age, see, and I think my size scares a few kids off even before a match. Have to grin when opponents point me out to each other as they're warming up. It's like giving us a goal start usually. But not today. I was playing like a lemon.

'Got something on your mind, have you, Everton Woods?' Sir said at half-time, dead sarcastic, you know.

Always a bad sign when Sir uses your full name. He hates us losing when he's ref 'cos he can't shout at us so much – just plods through the mud muttering to himself instead, getting all steamed up inside.

'What do you mean, Sir?' I asked, as if I didn't know.

'Looks like you'd rather be somewhere else.'

He was right in a way. For once, I couldn't wait for the school game to end, I was so excited. Why? 'Cos I was going to be Town's mascot in the afternoon, that's why! I'd won the Junior Supporters Club prize draw to be team mascot for the day, besides getting a new Town strip and leather football signed by all my favourite players.

Fantastic! Made a change to be able to boast about being a Town fan. Most of my mates support big famous teams like Man United, Newcastle and Tottenham, but they were well jealous, I could tell.

For a while yet, though, I somehow had to put all that out of my mind. I still fancied my chances of a goal or two in the second half. Their defenders were quite small, but I'd hardly had a decent header so far apart from one that grazed the crossbar. Nearly every centre had been reaching me about knee high.

'C'mon, try and get your crosses over higher,' I told the wingers.

It was no good. I didn't get my head to the ball much second half either. At first, I couldn't work out what was different about our opponents and then it clicked. They'd turned their whole team inside out!

'What's going on?' I asked the giraffe who was now marking me.

He grinned. 'Wondered how long it'd take you to catch on. It's the last match of the season and our teacher promised us all a bit of fun. Everybody's playing in different positions for a laugh.'

It wasn't a laughing matter for us. They played even better in their new line-up. Their captain had gone in goal and was gobbling up any ball we managed to get near him. And I'd also met my match in the air, I have to admit. The giraffe must have been the school's high-jump champion, the way he took off from the ground every time.

3

Three more goals went in at our end before Sir had finally had enough. 'Right, Everton Woods,' he stormed. 'You're off!'

For a second, I thought he was sending me off till I realized he was calling on a sub to take my place. I'd never been subbed before and it hurt, especially 'cos he seemed to be blaming me for the defeat. At least I knew my mates weren't. Bet they'd have given anything to be in my boots when I led the Town team out on to the pitch that afternoon.

I didn't hang around. I left for home straight away to get ready for the big match!

Guess with a name like mine, I've got to be a soccer nut, right? But it's got nothing to do with Everton Football Club. Dad's a cricket freak and I'm called after one of his old heroes, Everton Weekes, a West Indian cricketer from ancient history. You won't ever have heard of him, I bet. Came from Barbados, Dad's home island. The bloke's middle name was de Courcy, so suppose I should be grateful I escaped that!

Dad always takes me to watch Town play, though, and we've got seats up in the main stand. Daft, isn't it, when you stop to think about it? *Sitting* in a stand, I mean. People only actually stand when Town score a goal. I scramble up on my seat and cheer my head off.

Not that I've been getting much practice at doing that this season. Town haven't scored many and we were in danger of being relegated to an even lower division.

But not if I could do anything about it! As the mascot for the crunch game against the Wanderers, another team near the bottom, I was determined to bring them luck. We had to win to stay up!

Panic! Couldn't find my lucky scarf. Always wear it at matches to help Town win.

'Didn't think you'd need it this week,' Mum said. 'Not with having all that lovely new kit to wear. I've washed it.'

Washed it! Can you imagine? That's hardly lucky for a start. When I dug it out of the airing cupboard, I found the colours had gone and run. The gold was more like a dirty yellow now, but I still hung it round my neck. I wasn't going to be without it today, of all days.

It was an incredible feeling, I can tell you, trotting out of the players' tunnel on to the pitch next to the captain. The crowd might have been quite small, but their cheers were deafening. I strutted around in our smart green and gold kit, still wearing my lucky scarf of course, but pretending I was about to make my debut for Town.

I probably got carried away, wanting to show off, like. I passed a ball about with a few of the players and then smashed a couple of shots into the net. Just wish the keeper hadn't made it so obvious he was deliberately letting them in. I even tried to do some ball juggling, keeping it up on my feet, knees and head. OK, so I didn't get past a count of five, but I was kinda nervous in front of so many people.

Paul Fisher, Town's captain and centre-back, took me

up to the halfway line for the toss. I had my picture taken there and the ref gave me the coin, too, as a souvenir. In the end, it was a bit of a let-down when I had to leave the pitch and the match itself kicked off.

At least I was able to sit in the players' dugout with the Boss, the trainer and the subs, right up close to the action. Trouble was, Town got off to a terrible start, just like us in the morning. After only a quarter of an hour, we were 2–0 down and one of our defenders, Scott Bromley, had to come off injured with a pulled muscle.

He sat next to me on the bench, all miserable. 'Fine lucky mascot you're turning out to be!'

'Yeah, well, there's still time,' I mumbled. 'Anything can happen.'

'It already has, thanks,' he muttered, prodding his leg.

The Boss began to give me some funny looks as well. I returned a sickly smile when he caught my eye and just shrugged my shoulders, trying to give the impression it wasn't entirely my fault.

'So what are we goin' to do about this mess then, kid?' he sighed wearily. 'Pretty hopeless, eh?'

Wasn't sure he really wanted an answer, but I offered one anyway. 'Make some changes?' I suggested vaguely. 'Got nothing to lose.'

'Only my job,' he grunted and turned back to the game.

'Shall I go up and join Dad in the stand now and keep out the way?' I asked, but he ignored me.

Bromley spoke instead. 'What! Our *lucky* mascot wanting to desert the sinking ship!' he said, putting unkind stress on the *lucky*, I felt.

'No, I'd rather stay here and try to help, if I can.'

'Huh!' he mocked. 'Fat chance of that!'

Things did not get any better. In fact, just before half-time, they went and got a whole lot worse. Our keeper charged wildly out of his goal and clattered into an opponent as the player tried to dribble the ball round him. The referee pointed straight to the penalty spot.

He pointed towards the tunnel, too, showing the keeper the dreaded red card. The Boss jumped up to protest and smashed his head on the low dugout's concrete roof. It was a double blow. Town were down to ten men on the field and now had one less on the bench as well. The Boss was out cold!

While the trainer and club doctor took the Boss away, the players were left to sort out the goalkeeping problem themselves. We didn't have a sub goalie so Fisher pulled on a spare jersey to face the delayed penalty. That was the moment when we had our first piece of luck. Fisher never even had to make a save. He threw himself blindly to his left but got nowhere near the ball. It was ballooned way over the bar and dis-appeared among the spectators near the back of the terracing.

'How's the Boss?' asked Bromley when the trainer returned.

'Concussed. Doesn't even know what day it is, never

mind the score. What we gonna do?'

'Search me,' said the defender. 'It's up to you now.'

I saw my chance. It was either the most brilliant, inspired moment of my life – or the most stupid and reckless. I gulped and decided to risk it. Somebody had to try and do something to rescue the Town.

'Er,' I began, 'I think I know what the Boss was going to do in the second half . . .'

They turned to stare at me, only just about re-membering what I was doing there, judging by the looks on their faces.

'What d'yer mean?' demanded the trainer, his right eye twitching with the pressure of suddenly being left in charge.

'Well, I heard him muttering about making drastic changes at half-time,' I lied as the referee blew his whistle for the break.

'Right, lad,' the trainer said, grabbing me by the arm as Town's players trooped off the pitch, heads down. 'You're coming back to the dressing room with us.'

I didn't have any choice. I was led firmly down the tunnel, the trainer desperate to clutch on to any straw that he could. There was no backing out now. Somehow, I'd have to try and bluff my way through. My brain was racing even faster than my heart, rehearsing what to say.

Town's players were all sitting slumped on the benches around the room, drenched with sweat and staring blankly at the floor. All, that is, apart from the disgraced goalie. He was out of sight, and only the

sound of his running bathwater disturbed the silence.

'It's a good job the Boss can't get his hands on you useless lot right now,' bawled the trainer. 'But listen to young Everton here. He heard what the Boss planned to do before he got laid out.'

I swallowed hard and hoped that the players didn't notice how much my knees were knocking. I remembered how the school team had been fooled that morning by all those half-time switches and couldn't see any reason why Town might not do the same to the Wanderers. The water had stopped and my little voice seemed to echo around the walls as I found the courage to speak up. 'Things were so bad,' I explained, 'that the Boss must have decided to turn the whole team upside down.'

'Upside down?' the trainer interrupted.

'Well, back to front, then,' I continued, getting into my stride. 'Change everybody round and catch the Wanderers napping. Their keeper isn't very big, like our attack, and we haven't really tested him out in the air yet. We've got some dead tall defenders and they could play up front second half. The captain's wasted in goal in my opinion . . .'

Everybody looked gobsmacked. The players stared at me open-mouthed for a minute and then burst out laughing. The trainer eyed me suspiciously. 'Did the Boss say all that?'

I fidgeted uncomfortably in the uproar around me. 'Well,' I shrugged. 'Not all of it, maybe, I admit, but . . .'

'I don't believe it!' he stormed. 'You didn't hear him say anything of the kind, did you? What kind of a trick are you trying to pull . . .'

'Hold it!' exclaimed Fisher, jumping to his feet. 'Leave the kid alone, I reckon he's got something here. Even if he is making the whole thing up, it could be exactly what we need to do. The plan is so crazy, it's beautiful – and it just might work!'

The room came alive, everyone wanting to talk at the same time. The mood had changed completely, and so did the team for the second half as the players convinced the trainer it was a gamble worth taking.

'Oh, what the heck!' he cried. 'We were going to lose anyway. We may as well go down fighting. OK, lads, get out there again, guns blazing, and let's blast 'em!'

The ten players scurried out on to the pitch, keen to restart the game in their new positions. The crowd soon woke up to the fact that the winger was now in goal, but it took them and the visitors a bit longer to suss out the many other things that were different.

Poor old Wanderers never knew what hit them. By the time they'd managed to reorganize their marking system, we'd levelled the scores with two headed goals by Fisher. He and our lanky full-back were running riot in attack, causing total chaos whenever the ball was whacked high across into the box. This was no time for fancy, passing football. This was do-or-die, long-ball stuff.

With only ten men on the pitch, though, Town still

faced an uphill battle and it looked as if the Wanderers were going to hold out. A draw was no good to us. We needed all three points to avoid relegation. The trainer kept peering at his watch every few seconds and when we had a corner near the end, he waved the emergency keeper upfield as well to join in, leaving our goal totally unguarded. It was all or nothing!

Talk about panic! The appearance of our keeper's bright red top in their own penalty area caused the Wanderers all sorts of confusion. Two players ended up marking him and our giant, gangling full-back made the most of the distraction. He rose higher than anybody to meet the ball smack on his forehead and send it whistling into the net.

The Boss arrived on the scene just at that moment, still groggy. 'What's goin' on?' he cried.

'We've won!' I yelled back. 'We're safe!'

I was ecstatic! Three headed goals, just how I love to score 'em, and the celebrations after the match in the dressing room were amazing. Even the Boss joined in the party, despite his sore head, waving a glass of champagne around and spilling most of it.

As I sat on a table next to Dad, the Boss suddenly loomed up in front of me, a dopy, dazed kind of expression on his grinning face. 'Great win, eh, Liverpool?' he gushed.

'Everton,' I corrected him gently.

'Yeah, right. You'll have to be our lucky mascot every game, eh?'

I glanced at the trainer nearby. He put his finger to his lips and came over as soon as the Boss tottered unsteadily away. 'Don't say anything,' the trainer hissed. 'The Boss would have a fit and sack the lot of us, if he ever found out all those changes were your crazy idea.'

'Doesn't he know yet what really went on?' Dad gasped.

The trainer shook his head. 'Best to keep it our little secret and let the Boss take all the credit for the success. OK, Everton?'

I nodded and then smiled. 'On one condition,' I said cheekily.

'Name it,' he replied.

'How about you and a few of the players coming into school next season to give our team some proper coaching? It might even make my mates become Town fans as well.'

The trainer winked at Dad and shook hands with me. 'Done,' he agreed. 'You've got a deal, Everton. You deserve some reward for today – as long as the Boss never knows the reason why.'

What an incredible day! Guess that's perhaps why they sometimes say football's a funny old game. It must be when you can turn your team back to front and still win!

THE BLACK PEARL

by Jonathan Kebbe

Axeman always had it in for me. He's not racist. I think it just annoys him that God should have put so much natural grace into such a scrawny sap like me, who doesn't give a toss about winning.

The day he pulled me off in the semi-final, I was too upset to speak, and mitched school for three days. Peter Joseph McLynch – the player he sent on for me – scored the goal to put us in the final. I was finished.

Axeman (real name Mr Paxman; also known as Taxman, 'cos he fines us for swearing and losing kit) was always torn between me and PJ for the number nine shirt. PJ's a human giraffe, with meaty thighs and a strong neck. He scatters defences like a bowling ball, and plucks crosses from the air with his powerful head. I'm more like the runt in a litter of scarecrows, short and spidery, with knobbly knees and a soft head.

15

But I'm quick and cute, and I can do things with the ball no-one else can do. I can bend it round the best defensive wall, I can drop a fifty-foot pass in your lap, and mesmerize defenders like a snake.

But Axeman's mind was made up.

'You were useless,' he roasted me in front of everyone. 'This is big time, Limo. I need a raging bull up front, not a ballet dancer.'

No-one laughed. They know I'm good, and they knew I was hurt. So I had one of those games – I'm only human.

I nursed my pride at home, went for long winter walks with Georgie, my boxer (named after Georgie Best). Like Best, I'm Irish. Well, half-Irish, half-African. My ma's a district nurse. She fell in love with a young doctor from Nigeria. He missed Africa and family, and went home, breaking my mother's heart. All that's left of the marriage is me – Limo (real name Liam Millayo). They used to call me Half-caste and Caramel. They laughed 'cos I had no dad, and I'm brown in a white country, and my curly hair is reddish 'cos of my ma.

Then I got to know Sadie Costello. She showed me how to handle myself, cool like. She had her own battles. She was always trying to get into the squad.

'You need a decent sweeper, Sir.'

Axeman wasn't having a girl in his team, but she wouldn't give up. She'd ambush him outside the staffroom—

'Please, Sir—'

'I thought I told you to stop nagging me.'

'—give us a chance.'

'How many times do I have to tell you?'

'Just give us a chance.'

When Axeman was on playground duty, she made sure he noticed her by taking out boys with hideous tackles, 'cos that's the sort of thing he liked. But when it came to girls, he had a blind spot.

'Girls don't play football, Costello.'

'Just give me a chance, Sir.'

He slapped her in detention. She sat staring at him, her eyes saying loud and clear, Just give me a chance. He gave her one hundred lines of I MUST STOP PESTERING TEACHERS. She handed in five hundred lines of JUST GIVE US A CHANCE SIR.

Finally her patience snapped. She called him an extremely rude name, and got suspended for a week.

She lives on my estate, in the next block. We can see her da's window-boxes from our kitchen. She'd walk Georgie with me.

'Be patient,' I urged, 'that's what my grandad says.'

'Easy for him. I've tried everything. It's like talking to a wall.'

'Wrong, Sadie. You've got him saying he already has Duffy as sweeper. You're getting to him.'

'It's not fair,' she said, 'Duffy's gruesome.'

Sadie's ma died when Sadie was two. Her father brought her up to play football. The lads on the estate know she's skilled and hard – even if she is a Villa fan – and no-one complains when she joins in. No-one dares. She's like Georgie. Fight anyone.

When I wasn't in school after being substituted, she came knocking. Ma was at work, and my grandad was lost in a wildlife video. (He doesn't hear very well these days.)

'Why you off school?' Sadie said.

'Been sick.'

'Sick about Axeman giving your number nine shirt to PJ.'

'You're joking,' I laughed. 'I couldn't give a snot.'

I used to cry at night, when no-one could see me. I'm sick of being pushed around, sick of being laughed at. I miss my dad, I wish I was white. I'm sick.

'You're so stupid, Limo,' Sadie said. 'They only get to you because you let 'em.'

I laughed when she called me stupid.

'Yer, I'm stupid. Dada! Dodo!' I sang, making stupid faces.

But I was hurt. I like Sadie. Like her a bit too much. She's not exactly pretty, but she has fire and courage and laughs a lot, and I like being with her. I like her eyes, blue-green like Dublin Bay, with dark swooping eyebrows like a gypsy.

'You're lucky you're brown,' Sadie said. 'People would kill for a suntan like yours.'

'Lucky I got the body to go with it!' I said, flexing my monkey-nut muscles.

'You should be proud to be black. When they call you darkie, you should go, Yeah, man, that's me! I only wish I was dark as Pelé or Eusebio!'

'Who?'

'Never heard of Eusebio?' Shocked by my ignorance. 'Want to meet him?'

'Why, is he around?'

She took me home, and put on one of her da's videos. There he was, Eusebio, the black centre forward of Portugal, the most graceful player you've ever seen. Three-nil down to South Korea in the '66 World Cup, and he pulls the mighty Portuguese back from the brink with four out of five second-half goals.

Class!

'The Black Pearl, that's what they called him,' said Sadie, 'and that's what we call you from now on – Limo, The Black Pearl!'

'Nah,' I said, embarrassed, 'I just like playing. Maybe if I listened to Axeman—'

'Listen to me, you sap.' She fixed me with those sea-green eyes. 'You're special, you're an artist. Others play the game, but you *are* the game, and never let Axeman or anyone change you.'

A minor miracle occurred leading up to the final. Sweeper Duffy broke his leg on our frosty pitch. His parents weren't very pleased and threatened to sue Axeman. Axeman had more pressing problems. Who to play in Duffy's place?

We had our final league match that week. We'd already secured second spot, so Axeman wanted to use the game to find a sweeper.

Sadie marched into his office. On my advice she changed her plea from, Give us a chance, to a short speech ending with, 'If I'm no good, I promise I'll never bother you again.'

'You don't give up, do you Costello?'

'No, Sir.'

It was a grudge match against the school we'd pipped into third place. Me, I didn't even get on the pitch. And PJ rewarded Axeman by scoring the equalizer. But Sadie was a sensation. She distributed the ball with vision, and timed her tackles to perfection, harrying their strikers without fouling them.

Axeman went mad in the changing room.

'You were all pitiful. I've seen one-legged winos look livelier. Play like that next Saturday and you can kiss the Cup goodbye.'

Then he turned to Sadie, regarded her sternly. She sat dripping sweat, looking him in the eye. Everyone waited. You could tell the lads were with her. She'd hit a few reckless passes but she'd marshalled the defence like a veteran.

'Not bad, Costello. But you were dying towards the end. You're not fit.'

'I'll be fit, Sir.'

'In seven days? I doubt it.'

★

Axeman roared at us in the gym.

'Move it, Costello! What d'you think this is, a cat-walk? Don't hang on to it. It's a time bomb, not a bunch of daffodils!'

The pressure got to her. I could see her cheeks burning up.

'Stay cool!' I said, as we ran into each other. 'He's testing you.'

Axeman reserved his fiercest scorn for me.

'Call that a tackle, Limo? Looks more like a kiss. Get stuck in, you wimp!'

I've tried to do it his way, but my heart's not in it. Football isn't just a beautiful game to me, it's *the* beautiful game. To see Pelé suck the ball onto his chest and stroke a sweet volley; to see Roberto Baggio dance through a forest of hacking defenders to score like a swordsman; to watch Eric Cantona flick the ball up, like he'd conjured it out of his pocket, and lift it over the goalie like he's setting free a snow-white dove – that's football.

I don't care what team they play for. To me, they're all on the same side.

Axeman's version comes from another planet, where football is WAR! Kill the ball! Hammer the opposition! Smash-and-grab a goal, and now dig in and defend, defend! Plug the gaps and kick 'em, kick 'em! Ten minutes to go, waste time! Keep it in the corner. Stay down, lad! Make it look worse than it is – the whistle! We've done it! We've won! We've won! WE'VE WON!

The gospel according to the Axeman: winning is everything.

I'm sorry, Sir – I wanted to tell him – but I'd rather play football and lose.

I couldn't take any more. I went home on the eve of the final with Axeman's taunts ringing in my ears – I need men, Limo, not fairies. If you're too faint-hearted to tackle, I'm sure Miss McDermott could use you in her second-string netball team!

'Lay off him, Sir.'

'What was that, Costello?'

'You're too hard on him.'

'Who asked you?'

'He's brilliant.'

'Brilliant?' Axeman laughed. 'He was more like a bag lady today.'

'That's 'cos you've knocked the stuffing out of him.'

'I'm trying to put some stuffing back in him.'

'Then you're going about it the wrong way, Sir.'

'That's quite enough, Costello. Is this the thanks I get for giving you a chance to win your place?'

'You can stick my place,' she said, and walked out.

'Come back here, the pair of you!'

Our blood was up. We kept walking.

'Stop, I said!'

Axeman caught us up outside. Leaning on a gatepost, he took a moment to compose himself.

'Look, lads . . .'

'I'm not a lad, Sir,' Sadie said.

'You are if you're in my squad, Costello.'

'I'm a girl, Sir, and I can do anything a boy can do except pee in the air.'

Axeman blinked. Sighed. The things a dedicated teacher has to put up with.

'Look,' he tried again, indicating the dismal estates all around, 'it's tough out there, ask your parents . . .'

'Parent, Sir,' Sadie corrected him, 'we only got one each.'

'There you are. It's tough, and it's my job to prepare you for that tough world. If I'm too hard sometimes . . .'

Axeman hesitated. And my belly went all queasy, because he was trying to apologize.

'Things are hard enough, Sir,' said Sadie, 'without making them worse.'

All of a sudden he looked old and sad, and I felt sorry for him.

As I walked home with Sadie, PJ drew up on his bike.

'You're such a sap, Blackie. You've completely blown it.'

I saw red. I was ashamed, 'cos Sadie had stood up to Axeman, and I wanted to take it out on PJ, and I was about to drag him off his bike and bite him, when Sadie pinched me and hissed, 'Pride – remember?'

Yes. I'm black and I'm proud.

I shrugged and grinned at PJ. 'You better be good tomorrow, Cheeseface, 'cos I'll be waiting to come on and show you how it's done.'

'Better bring a cushion, Limo.' PJ gave a friendly

parting wave. 'You'll be needing it on that bench.'

Sadie's da was working, so she came home with me.

'Can Sadie eat with us, Mam?'

'So long as she doesn't expect a banquet.'

Ma produced a mountain of pasta in a sea of vege-tables.

'Oh, Mam,' I complained. 'I wanted a burger and chips.'

'There's ten times more goodness in this.'

'Your ma's right,' Sadie said. 'Or did you think Ruud Gullit has a McDonalds before a big match?'

'What big match? Who needs energy on a bench?'

'I thought you had a big final? Your grandad's look-ing forward to it . . . aren't you, Dad?' Ma called.

Grandad looked up from his paper.

'He's not picked me,' I tried to tell him, getting up from the table. 'PJ's going to play instead.'

Grandad frowned at the clock. He thought I said I was going to bed.

I slunk out. Sadie apologized to Mam and followed. The lift wasn't working, and on the way down I passed old Mrs Mulligan struggling up with her messages. Normally I'd stop and help, but I hated the world that night. Even when Georgie ran to me I ignored him, so he'd feel bad.

Sadie walked in silence beside me, biding her time. We could both feel the quarrel coming, and were wait-ing to see who'd start.

'Listen, Limo,' she rounded on me first.

But quick as a flash – 'Look, Sadie, I'm through with football. I'm going to take up something more suitable like skipping. Stay away from me. I'm only a wimp.'

'Do what you like,' Sadie snarled at me, all teeth and fire, 'but just remember something. You've been given the gift of magic, and you've no right to throw it in God's face. Also I hate it when you sulk.'

'Anything else?'

'Yes. Me da's working tomorrow, and if you don't show up to watch me, I'm never speaking to you again.'

I watched her grow smaller across the flats, hands in the pockets of her jeans. And I hated her.

I don't need you, or anyone.

I tossed and turned that night. Mam looked in.

'Can you not sleep, love?'

'Sure I can.'

'Mind if I sit down?'

'If you want.'

She sat close to me on the bed. She's tired out, and her hair's streaked with silver from worry and work. But she's still kind of pretty.

'Whatever happens, poppet, I'm with you. You know that?'

She touched my face, and it took all my concentration to stop the tears leaping out of my eyes.

Around midnight I got up and sat with Grandad, watching a programme about South Africa – some old black guy making a boring speech.

'Can you hear, Grandad?'

'Pardon?'

'Can you hear what he's saying?'

'Not really. A few words here and there.'

'Then why you watching?'

'I'm catching the man's spirit. In his face. You know who he is? Nelson Mandela. He had a gift to give the world, but he had to spend twenty-odd years in prison before they were ready for it.'

'What's his thing then?'

'Sorry?'

'His thing, Grandad, what's he about?'

'His thing is freedom. Your thing is football. Be patient. Your time will come.'

'I hope I won't have to wait twenty-odd years.'

I had a dream that night. My father flew in from Nigeria to see me play. He was tall and grey like Nelson Mandela. I so wanted to do well for him, that I tried too hard and had a brutal game. I couldn't control the ball. It kept spinning away from me. It took every ounce of effort finally to trap it, knock it up with my right and volley it in with the left. The net quivered with the force of the shot. I looked up to receive my dad's acclaim . . . and he wasn't there. I was alone on a stony beach. I looked round for the net. It was a clothes-line, a number thirteen shirt blowing in the wind. The ball had turned into a snowy cat, licking herself. The cat was Sadie. Looking at me. Daring me.

Saturday dawned bright and clear and cold. Sure, I

turned up. I was afraid Sadie really wouldn't speak to me again.

There was no bench, just a row of upturned orange crates for us, the subs. Axeman patted me on the head.

'Keep warm, Limo. I could be needing you.'

He was being nice. He had no intention of needing me. PJ was his man, and PJ looked good that day; tall, muscly and confident.

The opposition – league champions St Pats – were amazed to see a girl in our colours, and couldn't stop sniggering. And the ref wasn't happy, wasn't sure the rules permitted a female of the species on the pitch. Fair play to Axeman. No Sadie, he said, no match. The master from St Pats shrugged. He wasn't worried. He'd beaten us at home and drawn us away. His boys were the toast of Dublin.

As battle commenced, I felt a hand on my shoulder.

'Grandad, I told you, I won't be playing.'

He nodded and stroked my neck. 'I'm here to keep you company, son, that's all.'

I tried to give him my seat; he said he was too old to be a sub.

And look who else was here! Standing out from the crowd in her red beret and matching tights.

'Mam, I told you . . .'

'Mind your own business. I've come to support Sadie.'

An angry *Ooooh!* from the crowd made me turn to the match. St Pats weren't sniggering any more. Sadie had just scythed the legs from under their silky centre-forward. The game was barely a minute old, and the ref was waving a yellow card at her.

It was a gruelling first half. Their master and our Axeman share the same passion for war. Buckets of sweat, fierce shots, cracking tackles – the game had everything but someone who could calm things down, change the pace and weave new patterns. No budding Bobby Moore, no classy Cruyff, not even a cheeky Gazza.

PJ toiled up front, but they'd done their homework on him, and dogged his every move. Plus they had two giants in the defence. The Grim Reapers, we called them. They matched PJ blow for blow every time he went up for another hopeful cross.

To tell the truth, they were nearly all bigger than us. They came from the South Side, and looked like they breakfasted on raw lion.

Axeman went bananas at half time.

'Costello's the only man in the team,' he fumed, bringing an embarrassed snarl to Sadie's face.

Considering the opposition, you might have thought 0–0 was respectable.

'You're a load of ninnies! I want action! I want sparks to fly! I want blood! What do I want?'

'Blood, Sir,' droned the chorus.

Taking his life in his hands, our skipper, Mick 'Scalper' Rooney, piped up, 'What about Limo, Sir?'

Axeman never looked in my direction.

'You run the park, Rooney, I'll run the team. A bit more effort from PJ and we'll smash 'em.'

★

The second half echoed the first. Charge and counter-charge. Blood and thunder. Time and again, hostilities were suspended while young limbs and tender bones were treated.

Freezing on the touchline, I went for a walk behind our bawling, yelling supporters. Then I felt the tension in the crowd suddenly rise, and turned in time to see their nimble centre-forward plunge through a breach in our ranks to thump the ball past Spiky's outstretched fingers.

Axeman went red with rage.

'Where were you, Costello?' he hollered at Sadie. 'You're supposed to stop him, not wave him through. You're not picked to look pretty!'

Through all the whooping and cheering, Sadie caught every word. I saw the look on her face. The shame, the anger.

Time was slipping away. St Pats had bagged a precious goal and were falling back into defensive positions. Only earthworks and barbed wire were missing. PJ fought bravely, but he was tiring. His willing wingers were still sweeping over the crosses, but the Grim Reapers were waiting, one to mug PJ, the other to belt the ball away.

Axeman kept darting looks at his watch. Fifteen minutes. Plus whatever injury time. He had to do something. We were hurling everything at them to no effect. St Pats were cruising to a smooth professional win, a job well done and thumping celebrations on the coach home. And it seemed it could only get worse. Flushed with confidence, St Pats surprised us by streaming out of defence to release their lurking centre-forward with a long ball.

'Stop him, Costello!' Axeman bellowed. 'Take him out!'

Still smarting from her earlier humiliation, tiring Sadie set her sights on her man, and caught him from behind as he crossed the dreaded penalty line, cutting his legs from under him with one of the worst tackles I've ever seen.

No need for the crowd to bay OFF! OFF! No need for the ref to remind us that she was already on a yellow. Out came red, and Sadie walked, a twisted grin of hurt and pride on her face.

Axeman was livid.

'What are you trying to do, give it them on a plate?'

'What am I supposed to do?' Sadie shouted back. 'Ask him to slow down?'

While St Pats wasted time taking the penalty, Axeman threw feverish glances at me. I wouldn't look at him. I felt Grandad close by. Be patient, son. Your time will come.

Their skipper struck a clean penalty. The low shot sent Spiky through the air in the wrong direction . . . and hammered a post. Groans from the crowd. Flutters of relief. Still time to save it. Come on! come on!

'Limo!' Axeman called my name.

Like a losing poker player, he was ready to gamble

everything on his one remaining ace.

Number nine was held up to signal PJ's departure.

Number thirteen to announce my arrival.

Axeman was growling instructions in my ear. I didn't catch them. I could dimly hear school mates shouting encouragement, and I couldn't miss my ma's plaintive, 'Well done, Liam, well done!'

Mam, I felt like saying, I haven't done anything yet.

She's mad, my ma. She thinks I'm wonderful for just being in the world.

Shoulders drooping, PJ limped towards me and tossed me his hand. 'Good luck, Limo, you'll need it.'

As I strolled on to the park, I heard Sadie's bitter cry. 'Kill 'em, Limo, kill 'em!'

I don't think she really meant me to draw blood, but I caught her drift. Two glorious goals, that's all she wanted. That's all I wanted too. I wanted it for me Grandad, 'cos it would bring tears to his eyes. I wanted it for me ma, 'cos she's so alone, and I'm all she's got. And I wanted it for Sadie, 'cos I'm soft on her. If only I could seize this moment, maybe I could make her forget I'm small and spindly and have knobbly knees.

But I hadn't slept well or eaten much, and my bones were chilled. And anyway you can't change the pattern of a game in ten minutes. Yet I had to, because I knew the only hope of scoring lay in taking my time, and lulling their defenders into thinking I posed no threat. I'd never played against them, but they knew my reputation. Still, I didn't look much of a threat, slight and airy

31

and five feet nothing, and after a few minutes, I felt the Grim Reapers losing interest in me and relaxing. They had everything covered. I was nothing more than a fly in the ear. To remind me they were there, they clattered into me from time to time as I released the ball, leaving bruises for me to remember them by.

I could vaguely hear Axeman having hysterics on the touchline. He couldn't believe what he was seeing. One down in the final with minutes to go, and what's Limo doing? Sending and receiving pretty passes, like pass the parcel. I was meant to be making chances and trying to put one away. Instead I was feeding others, spreading the ball about like a Sunday knockabout.

The Reapers probably thought I was scared. But I was never less scared in my life. I was at home. I was where I'm meant to be. In a field or back lane, it's all the same to me. I may not be pretty off the pitch, but running with a ball, I'm beautiful. With a ball at my feet, I feel a rush of Celtic blood in my veins, I hear the pulse of Africa . . . I'm alive. I'm free.

The ball bounced and danced in and out of my feet. I toyed with it, teasing the Reapers, making them lean side to side like pine trees in a gale. I offered them the ball, tempting them to take it. They couldn't resist. They lunged like Cossack dancers, and I was away, leaping their legs like a gazelle. Twitching this way and that, I drew the last defender, and feigning left, I swerved right and hit a shot that only Jesus could have saved.

I heard the roar. More astonishment than joy. I saw

amazement on my teammates' faces, shock in the eyes of the Reapers. They had the perfect system. What went wrong?

I'm told Axeman was momentarily stunned, as if my shot had hit him in the head. Then he was running up and down the line, calling for greater effort. 'Four minutes, we can do it! Stick to the task lads, stick it to them!'

When I looked his way, he was waving a fist at me, afraid that now I'd scored, I might feel like taking a nap. More of the same he wanted. But I knew that wasn't possible. The Reapers were alive to me now, sticking to me like minders. And my teammates, convinced I held the only key to victory, kept returning the ball, like it was my property. What could I do, with the Reapers smothering me, elbowing me, riding on my shoulders? I wanted to vary the play, but we were ten tired sloggers, sliding towards extra time against stouter opponents.

Then, in the dying moments, Fate took a hand.

St Pats broke free in an attacking wave, overran our depleted defence, exchanged passes in our box and suddenly killed the game, leaving Spiky on his knees between the posts, beaten by a simple shot.

The hoots and roars briefly lifted the lid off the sky . . . and quickly turned to outraged booing. A brave linesman was cheerfully waving his flag. Offside. Disallowed. Free kick.

What followed happened so fast, it was over before the hissing had died down – the long high ball dropping out of the sky towards me, one of the Reapers closing on me like a maddened rhino, me trapping the ball with the left, spinning away with the right. One Reaper down, one to go, spreading himself to stop me. I jig left, right, left again, and in his panic he parts his legs, an invitation to poke the ball through and meet it on the other side . . .

The goalie's rushing out to close me down. I can hear the Reaper galloping after me, the crowd screaming, and I've a split second to juggle my options – lob the keeper or take the long way round – when a claw seizes my shoulder, and nearly tears the shirt from my back as I'm flung to the floor like an old coat.

The ref arrives in a sweat, stands to attention and flourishes his red card. The Reaper walks.

No-one wants to take it. They're all looking at me. Penalties are a cinch. Except under pressure. I hate that kind of pressure, but there was nothing for it. They're patting me on the back, I'm their champion.

It's me, the ball and the goalie.

It's easy really. I could do it with my eyes shut. But there's an angry hurt voice in me saying, Why should you? You're useless whatever you do. Your da didn't want you. Teachers despair of you. Sadie will never like you the way you like her. You're stupid and insignificant. Why not put it over? the voice tempts me. Teach Axeman a lesson. Show him you won't dance to his tune. Show the world you couldn't give a monkey's about winning.

It's a beautiful game, that's all.

I always take a short run up. Not even a run up. One, two crisp steps and *wham*! like a recoiling spring. The keeper, with bright top and fancy gloves, never moved. I could have put the ball over the bank and into the river. I don't know why, but I swept it past him into the net.

I was very quiet that night. I always am after that kind of game. The tension, the emotion, the relief.

Mam was so thrilled she could hardly keep still. Grandad took it all in his stride. 'Don't let it go to your head, Liam.'

How could anything go to *my* head?

Georgie rested his chin on my knee. He knew I was back.

Sadie came round, not knowing whether to laugh or cry. Sent off in only her second match.

'You were deadly,' I reassured her. 'It was Axeman's fault you got sent off.'

'You should have seen his face,' she said, 'when you hit them goals, and the way you took 'em.'

I did see his face. In the changing room. All smiles.

'Took long enough about it,' he laughed happily. 'I don't know, Limo. What are we going to do with you?'

'Got to admit, Sir,' said PJ. 'Limo was a bit special.'

I met Axeman's gaze.

I could see he was puzzled, asking himself, Is Limo a freak, or what?

Or what? That's the interesting question.

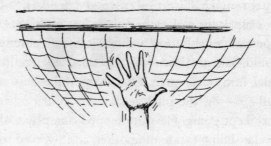

BANANA
by Neil Arksey

On Titch Wilson's eleventh birthday, his grandparents had given him a chunky black divers' watch. It was exactly the type he had always wanted; he was over the moon. After a huge lunch followed by chocolate cake, he and his sister Lisa set off home across the common.

It was the end of the summer holidays and the grass on the common was all dried up and yellowy brown from countless days of brilliant hot sunshine.

Shouting and swearing, charging around like headless chickens and angry rhinos, the boys from the neighbourhood were having a 'friendly' game. Clouds of dust swirled up from the ground as they pushed, barged and kicked each other and, occasionally, kicked the ball.

Titch stopped to watch.

The amazing Steve Bates was heading for the goal. Twisting – first this way, then that – he dodged effortlessly through half a dozen frenzied defenders. Still more ran to block his path, others were hot on his tail.

'On the wing, Batesy!' yelled Titch, suddenly spotting a slender shape down the far side, legging it like a maniac into open space. 'Out to the right!'

Others – on the pitch – shouted similar advice, but Batesy kept going. He side-stepped one player, skipped over the sliding tackle of another, and swerved to avoid head-on collision with a third.

Titch hurried along beside the action. 'Batesy!' he yelled, louder than anyone. 'On your RIGHT! Pass it out, you idiot. *Pass the ball!*'

Still Batesy kept going. It was impressive. He had gone round two more players and the goalie was coming out to tackle him. The lone winger had jogged to a stand-still almost directly in front of the open goal.

'Call for it!' Titch screamed to him. And then: 'Batesy, you big dope, pass the blinking . . .'

Too late! Batesy was down – a fair tackle – and the ball was being passed, fast and furious, back the other way. Batesy's side had been caught short, heading in the wrong direction. Now the opposition were running through.

As Batesy scrambled to his feet, at the far end a player was already whacking it home. There were loud cheers and hung heads – it had been the deciding goal. The game was over. Batesy's side had lost.

Batesy looked less than pleased.

'You!' he snarled, charging over. '*You* have just cost us the game, you little . . .'

'*What!?!!*' Titch looked round for support. '*Ref . . . !*'

'Your shouting and insults distracted me.' Batesy was standing right up against him, towering over, a head taller. 'Your stupid loud mouth's too big for your stupid little body!' Batesy shoved him hard in the chest.

'Oi!' Lisa yelled from somewhere behind. Titch stood his ground.

'Come on, Batesy,' he said, 'I only offered advice.'

'*You?*' Batesy laughed. 'Offer *me* advice?'

Titch nodded.

'When you can play as good as me,' said Batesy, jabbing a finger in Titch's chest, 'you can *maybe* offer suggestions. Till then – *shut it.*' Shoving Titch once more, he turned and stormed off.

'If you can't accept advice,' shouted Titch to his back, 'you'll never improve. And if you can't take losing, you shouldn't play.' Batesy had stopped in his tracks. 'Anyway,' added Titch, 'I'm as good a player as you, in my own position – and you know it!'

Batesy turned. '*Yeah?*' he sneered.

'*Yeah!*' said Titch.

'Don't make me laugh!' said Batesy. 'There's only one of us gonna be picked for the Coppice First Team this term – that's me and *you* know it.'

'Rubbish!' said Titch.

'Snot!' said Batesy.

'Wanna bet?'

'How much?'

'Er . . .'

'Come on – how much?' repeated Batesy.

Titch couldn't think. He'd never actually made a proper bet. 'This watch,' he said.

Batesy grabbed his wrist, looked at the watch and smiled. 'Done!' he said, shaking his hand like he wanted to wrench it off. And then he was heading off across the common, laughing and joking with his mates.

'Why are boys so stupid?' said Lisa, punching Titch, hard, on the shoulder. 'You included,' she added. 'If you lose your watch, you're for it, *Mr Hothead*. And you never even got him to bet you something in return. Coppice is a much bigger school than Daybrook Primary, you know. There might be others there better than you.'

Titch shook his head. 'Not in goal,' he said. 'I'm the best.'

The first few days at Coppice Hill School were non-stop. Titch's head span with all the new information – the lay-out of the classrooms and timetables, new subjects and teachers' names, school rules and routines. There were thirty new names and faces in his class – only six were familiar. There were four other classes in the same year.

Those who had been at Daybrook tended to come together at break. Batesy greeted him each time with a reminder about the bet.

'Hey – shrimp! Taking care of my watch? Looking forward to the trials?'

'You think you're such a big shot,' replied Titch, 'but which of us had the nerve to make the bet?'

*

Mr Drisco, the physics teacher, was in charge of the soccer team.

On the afternoon of the trials, boys gathered in the middle of the pitch. Mr Drisco marched out from the pavilion with his clipboard.

'Right!' he barked. 'When I call out your name, step forward and identify yourself. State what position you play, then stand in the appropriate line. Clear?'

Lines formed for each position. Hopeful strikers stood in the queue with Batesy, others lined up to be goalie, but the majority were going for midfield positions.

Titch's name was last on the register. When it was called, he stepped forward.

'Goalie, Sir!' he yelled.

Mr Drisco lowered his clipboard and peered over the top of his glasses, as if searching for the owner of this voice. Finally, focusing on Titch, he said sternly, 'You're pulling my leg, aren't you, Wilson?'

Laughter spread through the lines. Batesy's was, of course, by far the loudest.

'No, Sir,' said Titch. 'Goalkeeping is what I'm good at . . . Sir.'

'Well, a simple test should settle this,' said Mr Drisco. 'Goalies-to-be, follow me!'

There were seven other boys – three couldn't touch him, Titch knew for sure. He'd have to see about the rest.

'Right!' said Mr Drisco as they reached the goal posts. 'You are all going to jump for the crossbar. If you don't reach it straight away – keep trying. When you're ready . . .'

Titch froze. He knew he couldn't reach the crossbar. The others were jumping and Mr Drisco was staring at him, one eyebrow raised, as if to say, 'Well? What are we waiting for?' There was nothing else for it. He jumped.

'OK, OK – that's enough!' said Mr Drisco after a couple of minutes. 'Anybody, apart from Wilson, fail to make contact?' Too out of breath to speak, they all shook their heads. 'Very good,' said Mr Drisco. 'Wait here by the goal. Wilson, I suggest you join a line for another position.'

'But, Sir . . .' pleaded Titch, jogging to keep up with Mr Drisco. 'Sir, that's not fair . . .'

'Excellent jumps, Wilson, *for your height* . . .'

'Sir, I'm better than . . .'

Mr Drisco silenced him with a stare. 'You're too short,' he snapped, 'it's as simple as that. I'm not having someone goalkeeping for the team if they can't reach the crossbar.'

They had arrived back at the lines of boys. Batesy had a huge grin on his face, others were tittering. Titch had never felt so terrible.

Though he tried for a couple of other positions, of course he didn't have a chance. He had always played in goal – his skills were with his hands and body, not his feet. He could dive, he could catch and fist, he could even kick a ball, but when he tried to dribble or tackle, his feet got tangled up.

*

'So – how will you explain the missing watch?' said Lisa, as they walked home from school. 'Gran and Grandad will be heartbroken. Mum will *murder* you.'

'He's not getting it,' said Titch. 'The bet's not over till this term's finished. I watched the penalty shoot-out – the remaining goalies may all have been bigger than me, but they were rubbish. Sooner or later, Drisco will *have* to try me.'

Titch was a born goalie, he was a natural. His mum was forever complaining about how he couldn't sit still like ordinary people. He leapt around, throwing himself across the floor and diving for imaginary balls, even when watching the telly. His reflexes were second to none, his handling skills were excellent, his strength and speed – good as the best. The one thing he lacked was *height*.

This wasn't news to Titch – after all, everyone did call him 'Titch'. But it had never been a problem before – there had never been a crossbar. It had always been two posts, or two jackets on the ground, and if somebody kicked the ball above the goalie's reach, it didn't count. He'd always worked hard on getting extra lift, he could jump very high for his height. But not, according to Mr Drisco, high enough.

It had only been a matter of a few centimetres, certainly no more than six – Titch was sure he could soon gain that much. He started eating as much protein, fresh vegetables and fruit as he could. Chicken or egg sandwiches for lunch, fish or meat and vegetables for supper and, when his mum allowed it, he even ate cold leftovers – fish fingers or whatever – for breakfast. He cut down on the sweets, crisps and fizzy drinks, but drank more milk for his bones.

Every morning and evening he climbed onto a chair and hung from the top of the door-frame, letting himself stretch till his fingers hurt too much to bear. He did rope-skipping every day to increase his bounce, and swam as often as he could, because someone had told him it lengthened growing limbs. And, of course, he still practised his goalkeeping.

Batesy, meanwhile, was becoming less cocky with his mocking. Though the First Team had won at the start of term, it had not happened again. Plenty of goals were being scored by the forwards, but even more were being let in by the goalie. It was only a matter of time now. Mr Drisco, Titch felt sure, must soon offer him a trial.

But each week when, at the end of the physics lesson, Titch asked Mr Drisco if he could try for the First Team, the reply was the same:

'When you can reach the crossbar, Wilson, you'll have your chance.'

'But, Sir . . .'

'Wilson – I'm a physics teacher, a scientist, a man of reason . . . *till provoked*. Can you reach the crossbar?'

'No, Sir.'

'Then *cease*!'

Every day, walking home past the football pitch, Titch

jumped for the crossbar. Lisa checked for any progress.
The results were less than promising.

By halfway through the term, however, the First
Team's results were less than promising too. They
couldn't even manage a draw. Mr Drisco had tried playing the reserve goalie with no improvement in results.

When Titch once again made his plea to be considered for the team, Mr Drisco didn't take it too well.

'Wilson – you ask the same question every week.
Every week I give the same reply. I think your mind
must be too much on football and not enough on
physics.' Titch bowed his head. 'Next week, Wilson, in
front of the class, you will explain, using diagrams drawn
on the blackboard, the solution to tonight's homework
– exercise C. I want to see whether you *are* capable of
logical thought.'

Everyone turned to look at Titch.

'*In front of the class*, Sir?'

'Correct.'

'But, Sir . . .'

'*WILSON!*'

That was that.

Though he was a bit of a kidder, Titch was not the
sort that enjoyed getting up in front of people and doing
something *serious*. He dreaded the thought of being
laughed at and tended to make a mess of such situations.

Every night that week, instead of his usual training
and goalkeeping practice, he sat at home struggling with
the physics homework.

Lisa was shocked. 'What's come over you?' she said. 'You're never normally this quiet or still. It's really quite nice.'

But Titch was too busy working to reply.

The last night before it was due, he stayed up late checking and rechecking his work. At midnight, he leapt into bed, set the alarm and turned out the light. But, with his head full of circles and lines from his homework diagrams, he couldn't get to sleep. For a whole week he'd thought about nothing else. But now he was confident about doing those diagrams on the board tomorrow, old feelings of frustration about not being in the First Team began, once again, to nag.

Suddenly, he had a brainwave.

To reach the blackboard, he had to stand on tiptoe.

Having drawn two vertical lines, Titch joined them together at the top with a horizontal. Beneath he drew a circle and wrote: 'diameter – approx thirty centimetres'.

The class began to murmur and titter.

'Silence!' yelled Mr Drisco.

To the side of the circle, Titch drew a pin man with arms reaching up, the hands just a few centimetres below the horizontal line. The diagram was finished. Smiling with satisfaction, he turned to face the class. Mr Drisco was frowning, everyone else grinning.

Mr Drisco waved the sheet of homework questions and pointed at the blackboard. 'What,' he bellowed, 'is *that* a proof of, Wilson?'

'Sir, I've done all the homework problems,' said Titch, holding up his exercise book, 'but after I finished them, I came up with a proof of something else.'

Faces turned to see Drisco's reaction. 'Explain yourself!' he barked. 'Explain your diagram!'

'Well, Sir,' said Titch, gesturing at the board, 'as you can see – since a football . . .' he pointed to the circle '. . . is about thirty centimetres wide, a goalie . . .' here he pointed to his pin man '. . . does *not* need to be able to jump all the way to the crossbar in order to stop it. A goalie only needs to reach as high as fifteen centimetres below the crossbar in order to be able to stop *any* shot.'

You could have heard a pin drop.

You could have heard an ant sneeze (if ants had noses).

Mr Drisco scratched his head and stared at the diagram on the blackboard. 'Wilson,' he said, after a very long moment, '. . . would you be interested in trying for the First Eleven?'

The class exploded.

It was penalty shoot-out time again. Quite a crowd had gathered on the playing field to watch. Five players had been selected from the First Team, they were to take shots against each of three goalies: the main, the reserve and Titch. Batesy, one of the five, was arguing and shouting with the others in the centre of the pitch.

'You can't win, Batesy!' yelled Titch, from the goal. 'If I'm chosen for the team, you lose the bet. If I'm not, the team is doomed.' Batesy scowled and spat at the ground. 'But don't worry,' added Titch, 'I'm not letting *any* get past me!'

After the first three players had done their worst, Titch was smiling. Behind the goal, Mr Drisco was looking pleasantly surprised. Each of the other goalies had let in two, but he, Titch Wilson, had saved all three. If he saved the next one, he'd be in the team.

Walking out towards the penalty spot, Batesy looked ready to kill.

'This is it!' yelled Titch. 'Just you and me.'

Stony faced, Batesy placed the ball on the ground and paced backwards ten wide steps.

The crowd grew hushed.

Shaking his arms and legs one last time for looseness, Titch crouched low and focused his whole attention on the ball.

With a little skipping movement, Batesy began his run.

He was coming.

Faster and faster.

'*Grrrrrrrrrrrr!*'

He was growling.

Louder and louder.

He was *charging*.

As the outside edge of Batesy's boot made contact with the ball, suddenly everything seemed to slip into slow motion. It was like an action replay. Titch heard himself thinking, *It's a BANANA!* And sure enough, the

ball curved up and out before, gradually, as if pulled by some special force, it began to curl back. The ball was homing in on the top right corner of the goal.

Titch sprung, soared and – *yes!* – fisted the ball clear.

Jumping and cheering, the crowd swarmed towards the goal.

But what was this? He was still in the air! He could hardly believe it. *He was hanging from the crossbar!* And there, in the mob below, was Lisa – waving her arms, grinning and shouting. Mr Drisco and Batesy were pushing their way through.

'Very impressive!' yelled Mr Drisco.

Batesy looked up at Titch. 'Yeah,' he said grudgingly, '*very* impressive.' He held out his hand. 'But I bet you can't do *that* again.'

'Luckily, to save goals he doesn't need to,' said Mr Drisco. 'He's *proved* that.'

Titch dropped to the ground and grabbed Batesy's hand. 'No more bets,' he said. 'But we should shake hands as teammates.'

Batesy looked like he was trying to decide whether to snap Titch's elbow or yank his arm from its socket. His eyes, lingering on Titch's divers' watch, seemed suddenly to notice Mr Drisco's watchful gaze. 'OK, then' he said, managing the slightest smile, '. . . as teammates.'

Titch grinned.

And they shook.

UP THE PINKS!

by Emily Smith

It was Pru who came up with the idea. The four of us – Pru, Danielle, Rosie and me – were collecting our things from the side of the court after netball practice.

'It's *OK*, netball,' she said, pulling on her sweatshirt top. 'But it's not football.'

No-one was going to argue with that.

'I mean, let's face it, football is the game.'

I looked at her. 'The game?'

She nodded. '*The* game. That's what my dad says. *And* it's the national game. So why can't we learn football?'

There was silence. And then Danielle spoke.

'Hmm,' she murmured. 'It would be a good way to meet boys.'

We stared at her blankly.

'Boys? Who wants to meet *boys*?' I demanded.

'I do,' said Danielle. 'I'm in an all-girl family and an all-girl school. *I* want to meet boys.'

'But you wouldn't meet . . . *those* sort of boys playing

51

football!' said Rosie. 'It would be – you know – *grubby* schoolboys running down a muddy pitch with *grubby* balls clutched to their *grubby* shirts.'

'You don't—' Pru began.

'Well, *we'd* look pretty grubby, come to that,' I said.

Rosie bounced the ball against the netting. 'You don't meet boys playing football.' She grinned. 'You flatten 'em!'

'Trample 'em!'

'Mow 'em down!'

'You're not supposed to—' began Pru.

'Anyway, they'd probably flatten *us*!' said Danielle.

'No, they wouldn't!' I said indignantly. 'No way! We'd be a match at any game we put our mind to!'

Pru looked round at us. 'We're fit,' she said slowly. 'And fast. And brainy – you need brains to play football. But what about strength?'

'*I'm* strong!' I said. 'I'm as strong as any boy! You saw me kick that netball just now. I reckon . . . I reckon I could score straight from kickoff!'

'You can't—' Pru started.

But no-one was listening . . .

The next week Pru brought some of her dad's football books in. One wet break we sat around reading them.

'Look at that!' I said, holding up a picture of Ryan Giggs scoring.

'Way to go!' said Pru.

'He's cute!' said Danielle.

We ignored her, and studied the picture. Giggs was shooting low and hard into the net – the defenders were caught off balance, twisting towards the ball.

'Nice goal,' said Pru.

'Hmm,' I murmured.

'It's quite interesting . . . the tactics.' Rosie tapped a diagram in her book. 'You know, running off the ball and all that. It's more of a *tactical* game than I realized.'

'We'd be good at that,' I said slowly. 'We'd be good at tactics.'

There was silence.

'It'd be fun,' said Rosie.

'Great fun,' said Pru.

'And kind of interesting,' mused Danielle.

'Very kind of interesting,' said Pru.

'And different,' I put in.

'Quite different!' said Pru.

There was another silence. They all looked at me. And I said, 'Yeah!'

Danielle and Rosie nodded.

Pru grinned.

'Football, hmm? Football . . .' Miss Manister tapped the end of her pen on the dark wooden desk. She looked at us, considering. 'You really are serious about this?'

I glanced sideways at Pru, who just stood there goggling. She's no good with our head, Pru.

'Yes, Miss Manister,' I said in my most earnest voice. 'We really are serious.'

'Yes, Miss Manister,' echoed Danielle, and Rosie mumbled something at her end of the row.

'Hmm.' Our headteacher looked at us again.

'How many of you are interested? Enough for a team?' She gave a thin smile. 'Eleven, if I remember rightly.'

'Well, twelve with a substitute,' I said. 'And that would give us plenty of people for five-a-side.'

'Good practice, five-a-side!' squeaked Pru.

I nodded. 'That was Miss Barnes' idea.'

'Oh!' Miss Manister looked at me sharply. 'So you've talked to Miss Barnes, have you, Alison?'

'Yes, Miss Manister.'

'And what did she say?'

'She said—' I looked round at the others, and shrugged. 'She said OK, as long as you said OK.'

Pru grinned happily. 'She *likes* football!'

'I see,' said Miss Manister. 'Well, you've obviously given it quite a bit of thought.' She tapped her pen a bit more, and suddenly she nodded. 'All right! If you find eight more girls who want to play, *and* if you all get written permission from your parents . . .' She got to her feet. 'You've got your team.'

We filed out of her room, closed the door behind us – and gave silent whoops. 'Yey-*eh*!' whispered Pru, raising a clenched fist in the air.

'Eight more people . . .' I said thoughtfully, as we walked back to our form room.

'Shouldn't be too difficult,' said Pru confidently. 'Not if you take both classes in our year.'

'And not if we're involved,' added Danielle. 'People will be keen if we're involved.'

I nodded. After all, it was true . . .

★

'I've signed up Pat!' I cried excitedly, grabbing Pru and Danielle as they went into lunch.

'Great!' said Pru. 'She's big – we need a bit of size.'

'Excuse *me*!' Pat called from halfway down the lunch queue. But she grinned to show she wasn't really put out.

'What about Roxy? How did that go?' I asked, lowering my voice a bit.

'OK.' Pru laughed. 'She wanted to know if football was cool – you know Roxy. I said yeah – *dead* cool!'

Rosie joined us at the back of the queue. 'And I've got Lee – you know, the new American girl. She said wasn't football a bit rough?'

'Oh, did she?' said Pru. 'So what did you say?'

Rosie widened her eyes. 'I said, oh *no*, she was getting muddled up with soccer – and that football wasn't *at all* rough!'

We laughed.

'Sharon Baker said yes,' said Danielle.

'Oh,' I said, less enthusiastic. 'Do we *really* want Sharon?'

'Now, come on!' said Pru. 'Sharon may be a pain, but she's a games player.'

Rose nodded. 'Face it – she's our best netballer.'

I made a face. 'But *Sharon*,' I groaned.

'Now, look, Alison,' said Pru sternly. 'You can't just have people you like in the team – a team of Alison's mates.' She picked up a plate from the pile. 'We've got to have the quality.'

'OK, OK,' I said, rolling my eyes. 'Point taken!'

There was silence. Rosie peered ahead of the queue to try and see why it was taking so long.

'Salad!' said Danielle shortly. 'Salad always takes ages.'

Rosie nodded. 'So it looks as though we'll get our eight,' she said.

'Easily!' said Pru. 'It'll be more a problem sifting out the rubbish.'

Danielle was drumming her fingers on the metal runners. 'I was just wondering . . .' She frowned. 'What shall we *wear*?'

'Oh, nothing!' said Rosie impatiently.

'Great!' Danielle rolled her eyes. 'A naked girls' football team – *that* should be interesting!'

'You *know* what I mean!' said Rosie. 'Just our normal games kit – nothing special.'

'Nothing special?' cried Danielle. 'All this work talking to the Manister and being nice to Sharon Baker and all this training we're going to do – and we don't get to wear something *special*?'

'I agree with Danielle,' said Pru suddenly. 'I think we should have something!'

'OK,' I said. 'What about red? That's our school colour.'

'Man United are short-sighted,' sang Pru.

Danielle wrinkled her nose. 'Not red,' she said. She looked at us and grinned. 'Pink?'

'*No!*' we all shouted. 'Not *pink*!'

There was silence, and then Pru said thoughtfully. 'I don't know, though. What *about* pink? After all, we could probably swing it, being close to red.'

I stared at her. 'You can't be serious. Pink? It's so . . .

so girly!'

She grinned. 'Well, why not? Put the opposition off their guard.'

'A sort of bluff,' said Rosie.

Pru nodded. 'Pink and *mean*.'

Hmm, I thought to myself, as I started to help myself to the salad. Why *not* pink?

I speared a bit of ham on my fork. Then I turned and grinned at the three of them. 'Up The Pinks!' I cried, whirling the ham round in the air. 'Up The Pinks!'

So we started training.

Barnesy, our P.E. teacher, was great – really great.

She made a neat five-a-side pitch, and marked up a full-sized goal on the bottom wall so we got practice shooting.

Her last school was mixed, and she'd taken football there. And, as Pru said, she *liked* football!

She didn't have any time for slackers though.

'Come on, *move*!' she'd shout. 'Five-a-side's no good unless you play it fast. And I mean – fast!'

So we played it fast.

'And put more vim into those tackles!'

So we put more vim into the tackles.

'And *try* to stop handling the ball!'

So we tried to stop handling the ball. (In fact everyone got out of it pretty quick, except Pat when she got excited.)

A few people dropped out after a bit, but they were the unkeen ones anyway. We were left with the ones we wanted. Well, mostly the ones we wanted.

Sharon Baker kept playing.

In fact Sharon turned out to be a bit of a football star – good balance, good tactics, good stamina, the lot. She was a bit mean with the ball, though. She liked to keep it to herself rather than pass – she was *that* sort of player.

One of the things Miss Barnes got us to do apart from five-a-side was called 'sprinting after a goal kick'.

It only took three people, and how it worked was this. One of us would take a goal kick from the goal, getting the ball as far away as possible. The other two would have to wait on the goal line until the ball was kicked. Then they'd sprint after it, grab the ball (no hands, of course) keep possession, and try to score a goal. If they were successful, they'd take the goalie's place and do the goal kick.

It was hard work, I tell you.

And it was hardest work of all against Sharon. She had all the tricks up her sleeve – dummy runs, the lot. And sometimes she would give this annoying snicker when she beat me. But that just made me try harder . . .

'Well done, Sharon!' said Barnesy one afternoon, coming over after another Sharon goal. 'You're coming on nicely. Very nicely indeed.'

Sharon looked dead pleased.

Barnesy turned to me. 'And you've got a good technique, Alison. You're going to make a very useful striker.'

'Yeah?' I said, delighted.

Barnesy nodded. 'Yes. Remember to keep your head over the ball, though.' She looked at Rosie, strolling up with the ball under her arm. 'Not bad,' she said, 'but we'd better do some more work on goalie skills. You seem to be holding your hands a bit funny.'

Rosie shrugged. 'OK!' she said, quite happy.

Barnesy smiled and turned to go.

'Miss Barnes?' I called.

She turned. 'Yes?'

'When – when are you going to place people?'

'Hmm.' She pursed her lips. 'Quite soon – I've got a pretty good idea now.' She paused. 'We need a captain too, of course.'

Sharon looked at her. '*I'm* captain of the netball team,' she said.

'You are, Sharon, you are,' said Barnesy. But she didn't say anything more. She just smiled at us two and dashed off.

Rosie and I looked at each other. We knew what Sharon had in mind! And we weren't having it! We raced in to find Pru and Danielle.

'No way am I playing in a team with Sharon as captain!' I said fiercely, when we'd explained it all.

'She is good,' said Pru doubtfully.

'That's not all to being a captain,' said Rosie.

'No,' agreed Danielle. 'And I'm not sure Sharon *would* make a good captain. She's all sort of – out for herself. She won't encourage Pat and people like that.'

'I think one of us four should do it, anyway,' said Rosie. 'One of us should be captain.' She frowned. 'And I think that's what Barnesy thinks too.'

There was silence.

'Pru?' Rosie suggested. 'Pru for captain? After all, it

was all her idea.'

'Alison?' suggested Danielle.

Pru and I looked at each other. We both knew that it was between us. We both wanted it. And then Pru drew breath.

'Alison would make a good captain,' she said slowly. 'She's good, and she . . . well, she's the sort of person to get the best out of the others. I know Barnesy would agree.'

Danielle met Rosie's eyes. And suddenly it was decided.

Rosie banged me on the back. 'Congratulations, skipper!' she said.

'Game on!' said Barnesy with a grin at the beginning of football practice that Thursday.

'What?' I said.

'Game on,' she repeated.

'You've fixed up a *game*?' said Rosie.

She nodded.

'Who with?' said Danielle.

'Eccleston,' said Barnesy. Eccleston was the boys' school the other side of town.

'Wow!' said someone.

'Who *exactly* at Eccleston?' said someone else.

'Same year as you,' said Barnesy. 'The B Team.'

'Cheek!' said Sharon Baker.

I shook my head at her. 'Come on!' I said. 'It's our first game!'

There was silence.

'Our first game!' said Rosie, softly.

'Our first game,' said Pru, grimly.

'Our first game,' said Danielle, grinning.

'Our first game,' I repeated.

Danielle frowned. 'We must get on with our kit!' she said.

'Up The Pinks!' said Pru, grinning.

'Up The Pinks!' I echoed. 'Up The Pinks – I hope!'

The twelve of us climbed out of the minibus at Eccleston.

We looked at each other. This was really happening! Even Sharon Baker seemed less confident than usual. And little Janice Sharpe, one of our midfielders, looked liked she was gibbering.

'Come on, team!' I said, remembering my role as captain. 'Let's go and mash 'em!'

A P.E. teacher in a purple tracksuit came out and greeted Barnesy – then he led us round the back of the school.

There, in front of us, was the pitch (looking *enormous*) and the opposition (not, thankfully, looking *so* enormous). They were doing warm-up exercises.

A tall fair-haired boy came up. (Danielle was so phased, she didn't even murmur 'cute'.)

'Our captain, Mike,' said the Eccleston teacher.

'And ours, Alison,' said Barnesy.

We nodded at each other.

'Right, girls,' said Barnesy. 'Let's get going.'

We stripped down to our pinks, and did some

61

knee bends and stuff.

'OK, team,' I said after a minute. 'Fit?'

'Yes!' said everyone.

'Ready to go?'

'Yes!' said everyone.

'So go out there – and win!'

'Yes!' said everyone. Everyone, that is, except Pat.

'Do we really want to win?' she said.

'YES!' we all yelled.

'But look at them,' she said, surveying the blue shirts. 'Look at those boys. They'd be so *pleased* if they won.'

'Pleased?' I shouted. 'Pleased?' Here we were, at our first match, and Pat, the mainstay of our defence, was going soft on us!

'Now look, Pat!' I cried. 'We're here to win! Look over there!' I pointed to two boys talking on the touch-line. 'I bet those two are sniggering away saying girls can't play football!' (I didn't actually think any such thing – I was just trying to rouse Pat.)

'Well?' Pat shrugged. 'They're entitled to their opinion.'

'Entitled to their opinion?' I yelled. 'Of course they're not entitled to their opinion!'

But there was no time for more pepping up. It was time for the match. Dressed in our pink strips, we jogged into position. We were playing four-two-four, with Rosie in goal. Sharon and I were to lead the attack, backed up by Danielle and Roxy, Pru and Janice were in midfield, and Pat and three other players were in defence.

The Eccleston P.E. teacher was refereeing the first half, and Barnesy was doing the second.

We won the toss, and I chose to kick off.

The whistle blew and we were away! I did a nice kick upfield, and Sharon quickly trapped the ball. Straightaway she tried to force her way through a crowd of Blues.

Not surprisingly she lost the ball after a bit, and soon it was making its way back up to our goal.

The Blues were eager for a goal – there was no doubt they were trying. They didn't expect us to be a walkover. I suddenly thought – let's hope we're *not* a walkover!

They got past Pat and the other defence players quite easily, and suddenly my heart leapt into my mouth. I realized that one of their strikers, a stocky dark-haired boy, was preparing to shoot.

He gave it a good shot. It was wide – but only just. And I knew then that it was going to be a hard match . . .

The ball stayed our end of the pitch for a bit, and then the dark-haired boy, who seemed to be everywhere, trapped it close to the touchline.

He tried a centre towards the edge of the area, but somehow it went out to the wing. Pat lolloped up to take it – and just didn't get there. She's never the fastest player (she's strong and accurate – but *not* fast), and right now she hardly seemed to be trying! A Blue beat her to it, and kicked the ball towards the penalty spot. Mike was waiting in just the right place to ram it into the net. One down already! I was choked!

We trooped back to our positions. I wondered whether to have a word with Pat, but before I could make up my mind, it was too late.

I needn't have bothered anyway, after what came next.

We managed to get the ball upfield again by short quick passes to any pink shirt in sight. Then Danielle took the ball and passed it quickly to Roxy (Sharon was yelling for it, but she took no notice of her). Roxy dribbled nicely towards the goal, dummying past two Blues, and then passed quickly back to Danielle – who had dashed towards the Blues goal. And then – the whistle blew for offside!

Oh no! I thought. And Danielle looked as though she could have kicked herself. Sharon was shaking her head at Danielle – but it wasn't really her fault. You don't have offside in five-a-side football, and even though we'd watched all these videos at Pru's house, it's difficult to remember these things in the heat of the battle.

The Blues full-back took the free kick, and cleared it up the right wing. Pat started lumbering towards the ball – a split second too late as usual. Three Blues converged on her – and then something happened. A foot shot out, and the next minute Pat had gone headlong into the mud, while the Blues just charged on with the ball. No whistle went – it all happened so quickly, and Pru was blocking the view of the referee. So the Blues' striker got in position, and smacked the ball in. Rosie tried a flying save, but she just couldn't quite get there.

Two down! The Blues were grinning. I looked at Pat, climbing slowly to her feet – and looked again. Her face

64

was as black as thunder! She was a different person! She was *mad*! My heart leapt! Our full-back was back in the game!

After that we had a defence. And we needed one! The Blues were playing a strong game – not tactical, perhaps, but strong. I couldn't help feeling pleased we weren't playing the A Team!

We did get the ball up to their end a bit, though. And there was one funny moment after a free kick. Danielle found herself with the ball, and with no-one in the goalmouth. She tore towards the goal.

The Blues' goalie came out to narrow the angle, his arms spread wide. He came out too far in fact, and Danielle rushed on and on – straight into his arms! The ball bounced harmlessly over the dead-ball line, and I grinned at Pru. 'Well,' I remarked. 'She said she wanted to meet boys!'

Ten minutes later I wasn't grinning. The Blues scored their third goal after two Pinks crashed into each other, and Rosie leapt just too late. And then the whistle blew. It was half-time, and we were three goals down.

We ran over to Barnesy, depressed.

'Well done, girls!' she said brightly.

'What do you mean, well done?' I asked. 'We're three goals down!'

She smiled. 'I mean well done! You're giving them a game – and I'm proud of you!'

'You are?' said Pru, surprised.

'I am,' said Barnesy.

We looked at her, and saw she meant it.

I don't really know what happened in the second half. Maybe it was because Barnesy was pleased with us and she was refereeing. Maybe it was because we really were fit – and the boys were flagging. Or maybe it was just that we suddenly got it together as a team. But for whatever reason, the game started going our way . . .

Pat got a great tackle in early on, and played the ball to Pru – who slipped it to Janice. Janice and Pru did a textbook wall pass, and then Janice hit a long ball towards goal. I reached the ball first, just in the penalty area. The ball bounced in a really weird way, and I only half sort of hit it. But it curled over the goalie's head, and then bounce, bounce – it was in by the far post. GOAL! GOAL! Our first ever goal! I nearly exploded with joy!

The next was Sharon's. Pru played a beautiful cross to her feet, and she let fly in style. The ball went in just under the crossbar. GOAL!

The Blues came back then with a vengeance. And we only just managed to keep them off. Rosie did some good saves. And I have to admit we were really lucky at times.

Once one of their own men got in the way of what looked like a certain goal.

A Blues' midfielder shook his head, and said to Mike, 'Huh! Beginners' luck!'

Trevor replied. '*And* how!'

'Nonsense!' I shouted at them. 'It's skill, boys. Skill!'

And Mike grinned at me.

The next time we got the ball, Pru got past two Blues and squared the ball to Sharon. Sharon looked as though she wanted to keep it, but three Blues bore down on her, and she played it back again. Soon Pru was racing well with the ball.

She paused before the goalmouth, and shot hard. The Blues' goalie plunged sideways and knocked the ball into the air.

I tore up as the ball spun in the air. It was too far! I couldn't reach it! And then I did something I'd never done before, and I'd only seen on video. I took off in a full-length dive and headed the ball – right into the back of the net!

GOAL! Three–all, and we'd equalized! I just lay there. I knew I should get up, but I couldn't. I just lay on the ground, my forehead still feeling the blow, thinking about what I'd just done.

Finally we staggered into positions. We had about three minutes to stop the Blues doing any damage – and we managed it. WOW!

'Up The Pinks!' we shouted in the bus on the way back. 'Pinks for ever!'

'We are the champions!' shouted someone.

'We are the champions!' shouted everyone.

'Hang on,' said someone else. 'We only equalized!'

'Yes,' I said with a grin. 'But face it – we were ruddy marvellous, weren't we?'

'Up The Pinks!' we shouted, as the minibus pulled up at school. 'Up The Pinks! Up The Pinks! Up The Pinks!'

AS LONG AS IT TAKES
by Dennis Hamley

Some said Jason spent too much time in the other side's penalty area.

'You rotten goalhanger,' opponents would shout.

'Look son, you're offside so often you make other teams look more boring than Arsenal,' said Dad.

'Think of it this way,' said Mr Jenkin who looked after the school team. 'In any twenty-four hours a stopped clock is only right twice.'

'Don't you worry,' said Grandad. 'Twice is quite enough in a game of football.'

Jason agreed with Grandad. He was always hearing about strikers getting in good positions. Why bother? he reasoned. Why not *be* in the best position and stay there? Several times that season he'd shown that twice was quite enough. So Winsley Junior School was top of the Schools District League. If they won their next match against Costers Park then they need only draw in their last against their chief rivals, Feldover. If they drew – well, then it didn't matter what happened. Feldover would have to win 9–0 in their last but one game to have a better goal difference.

'Jason, if I could make you move round a bit more, you'd be a really good striker,' said Mr Jenkin.

I'm more your elegant, laid-back type thought Jason, but didn't say it.

It was all right in practice. With Mr Jenkin bellowing, Jason ran round like a scalded cat. The trouble was, *he* knew he was always out of touch then. When he played like he wanted to, then he was, just now and again, *devastatingly* in the right place. And the moment he pulled the Winsley shirt on and stepped out onto a spectator-lined pitch, he knew he was going to revert to type.

'Don't listen to them,' said Grandad. 'You're all right as you are. You're years before your time.'

Jason liked listening to Grandad. He lived just up the road. Jason often went round for moral support. After all, Grandad had been a useful striker in his day – even if he did prefer to call himself a centre-forward.

The night before that penultimate game against Costers Park, Jason was at Grandad's again. Nan was out. They sat each side of the fireplace, still glowing with an open fire, and Grandad talked.

'You're doing it the right way, Jason,' he said. 'It's no use charging round dementedly. If you just slow down and *watch*, you'll learn where to go to be effective.'

Behind Grandad was a glass cabinet full of little silver cups, medals and statuettes, which he, not Nan, polished every day. Jason loved looking at them. Winsley United's triumphs through the Forties and Fifties. Yes, Grandad had been pretty good over all those years.

'Have you seen this one?' said Grandad. He took out a silver medal: COUNTY MINOR CUP 1948 WINSLEY UNITED JOINT WINNERS.

Jason didn't remember it particularly.

Grandad was straightaway into reminiscence.

'That's when I learnt the real lessons about being in the right position,' he said. 'Because of Porritt, goal-keeper extraordinaire. Ah, Porritt. What a man! Have I told you about when I played for Winsley United Minors?'

Jason was puzzled.

'How could you?' he said. 'There's no pits round here.'

'Under eighteens, you twerp,' Grandad replied.

Jason cast his mind back over the many stories. No, he couldn't remember the Minors. Or Porritt.

'I was seventeen,' said Grandad. 'Us Minors – we were good. Made a change for Winsley folk. The grown-up team was rubbish.'

Jason looked over Grandad's shoulder at the trophy cabinet.

'Oh no, lad,' Grandad said. 'The team got better as we got older. Anyway, that year we were in for the County Minor Cup. Round after round, we beat everybody out of sight. Our first taste of glory. We had big crowds coming to see us play at home, the brass band out playing at half-time. The first team never had them. We got to be a right big-headed lot.'

And why shouldn't you? So will we if we win that league, thought Jason.

'So up came the final. Big stuff. Thirty miles to a professional ground. Stands and terraces and proper dressing rooms. The biggest day of our lives. And guess who we were playing. Feldover Minors.'

'That's who we're playing in our last match,' cried Jason.

'Well, history always repeats itself,' said Grandad.

'Go on,' said Jason.

The phone rang. It was Nan. She wanted Grandad to pick her up from her Women's Institute meeting.

'Got to go,' said Grandad. 'I'll run you home. And I'll tell you about the final and Porritt the goalkeeping prodigy next week.'

The following day, Mr Jenkin drove Winsley Juniors to Costers Park in the school minibus.

It was not Jason's day. Two ways of playing were fighting it out in his head – Mr Jenkin's and Grandad's. First, he ran and ran and tried to work hard and was never quite there with the play. So he slowed and watched and waited. And got offside again.

They were two down at half-time. Mr Jenkin tried very hard to be patient.

'You shouldn't be trailing,' he said. 'You've got the beating of them.'

'It's Jason's fault,' said Darren.

'He's rubbish,' said Dilip.

'Take him off, Sir,' said Terry.

'I'll do no such thing,' said Mr Jenkin. 'He must sort himself out. And you must help him. Think of the games he's won for us.'

'A goalhanger who gets lucky,' said Errol.

Jason was stung.

'Then I'm lucky a lot,' he said spiritedly.

'Just cool things, all of you,' said Mr Jenkin. 'Now, get out there and *do* it.'

It looked as if they would. Three minutes from the restart, Terry made a run down the left and crossed. Jason, like the stopped clock at ten past eleven, was exactly right and buried the ball in the net before the Costers Park goalkeeper could move.

Parents who'd made the trip went wild. Mr Jenkin shouted, 'That's more like it. Now, *play*.'

And they did, out of their skins. The trouble for Jason was that Mr Jenkin seemed right and ten past eleven only comes once each morning. It took a sweating, red-faced Darren to equalize ten minutes from time.

So – ten minutes to make the League safe and the Feldover game just a celebration. They strained themselves to do it. Every Winsley player bar Puggy Thorpe in goal piled into the Costers Park half.

'Watch for the breakaway,' shrieked Mr Jenkin.

It came. A desperate clearance found a Costers Park forward clear of everyone.

'*Offside*,' shrieked Dilip, Errol and Darren in unison.

The referee waved play on.

'He's in his own half,' shouted Mr Jenkin. 'Get on with the game.'

And they had to, desperately. The whole Winsley defence had to turn round and gallop back after three Costers Park forwards.

'Three against none,' groaned Mr Jenkin. 'After all I've tried to tell them.'

They bore down on Puggy. Mr Jenkin closed his eyes. So did nearly everybody in the Winsley team. They waited for their opponents' appalling shouts of joy.

They never came. Cautiously they all opened their eyes. Puggy lay prone on the ground. Injured? Where was the ball?

Puggy got up. He had been shielding the ball with his body. He bounced it, took two paces, hoofed it into the Costers Park half, walked back to his goal and said complacently to the surrounding spectators, 'You can watch *Match of the Day* all season and not see a better bit of goalkeeping than that.'

Alone among Winsley players, Jason had kept his eyes open. He'd seen how perfectly Puggy had timed his run out of goal, what guts he had in not flinching, how perfect was his dive at the feet of the rampaging Costers Park striker, how safely he had fallen and shielded the ball. What had Grandad said? Goalkeeper extraordinaire?

74

Prodigy? This Porritt couldn't be a patch on Puggy.

'Wake up, Jason.' Mr Jenkin's bellow made him jump.

He was standing in his favoured spot just by the penalty spot. Puggy's clearance had been helped on by Dilip. The ball was flying towards him. Bring it down, a quick turn and . . .

The whistle blew. Whether the Costers Park defenders had meant to pull a perfect offside trap no-one knew. But they had, and Jason had fallen right in it.

And that was it. Full time, two-all and the League looked just about safe. But Mr Jenkin had borrowed a parent's mobile phone and came in to tell his team the bad news.

'Feldover won nine-nil,' he said. 'So it's win or nothing next week, my lads.'

It was a gloomy ride home in the minibus. Jason was not very popular.

'I was going to tell you about the Minor Cup Final, wasn't I?' said Grandad. 'And Porritt the Great.'

Jason hugged his knees. He'd been waiting all week for this. It would keep his mind off tomorrow's game.

'Oh, it was a big day all right,' said Grandad. 'A perfect May evening: clear, sunny, dry pitch, no wind, packed ground. That was a brave sight for us, to walk out onto that. A lot of us wondered whether it forecast great things to come. People in Winsley had hired every coach in three coach firms; seeing the car-park full of packed coaches like when you go to big League games was really scary. And what the two lots of supporters were shouting at each other! I remember one little Winsley lad yelling at the Feldover lot, "Have your players got stinkbombs down their pants or is that just natural?"

'Who was that?' said Jason, storing it away for the future.

'Your Uncle Ernie,' said Grandad.

Uncle Ernie was an undertaker and spent most days wearing a black suit and pious expression. Jason was awed at life's unexpectedness.

'If he said it nowadays he'd be lynched,' said Grandad.

'Get on about the game,' said Jason.

'Well, it was time: the teams came out together. We were in our usual red and white stripes. They had green shirts with white sleeves, Arsenal style. And for the first time I saw Porritt.'

He paused. 'Go on,' said Jason.

'Well, he'd make any striker's heart sink. He was only seventeen, but he was nearly seven feet tall and no bean-pole with it. When we were warming up I looked at him. He made their goal look half the size of ours. He was plucking the ball out of the air as if he was playing with toddlers. The mere sight of him looked worth three goals a game.'

He was quiet again. Jason could see these memories were very clear.

'We soon saw how they'd got to the final. They had

the perfect game plan. It wasn't only their shirts which were Arsenal style. We had all the play – in their half all the time. They defended like mad and didn't worry about how many mistakes they made. Porritt was always there to get them out of trouble, so easily. And you had to watch them on the break.'

'And did you?' said Jason.

'Of course,' said Grandad. 'We hadn't got to the final through luck either. We were good. We should have caned them at least four-nothing. But they had Porritt.'

Grandad kept lapsing into dreaminess, as if he had to re-enact the memories before telling them. Jason waited impatiently.

'I was centre-forward,' he said. 'I was a good striker, like you. But people called me slow. I always said I didn't need to be fast. I read the game.'

'Like me,' said Jason.

'It takes learning,' said Grandad. 'But Porritt taught me something. I wasn't top scorer year after year for nothing. Big clubs came to see me, you know.'

Yes, Jason did know. 'Go *on*, Grandad,' he said.

'It was soon me versus Porritt. He made high balls look so easy. Most goalkeepers his height can't get down on the ground easily. Not Porritt. He was agile like a monkey. You couldn't chip him, you couldn't lob him, it was no use going for the corners – he just lazily took the ball in those huge hands wherever it came. He ate crosses for breakfast. He closed you down when you tried to dribble round him as if you weren't there. He made me *sick*. And he was so *graceful*. Like a ballet dancer, a cat. I can still see him. He was *incredible*.'

Now Grandad was silent a long time, remembering. Jason never asked him to go on. He was seeing Porritt as well.

'There was no score at half-time and we should have had at least three. I had to work out how to beat him. We talked over ways, tried them in the second half, got nowhere. And they didn't work in extra time either. Goalless draw. We had to come back for a replay next week.'

'A week to think out what to do,' said Jason.

'Yes,' said Grandad. 'The thing was, he commanded his penalty area so much that as soon as the ball got there you *assumed* he would get it. So did he. Which was *why* he did. Was there any way of putting him off balance, making him hesitate a bit? Well, we worked a few things out.'

'And you tried them in the replay.'

'Hold on a minute. I've got to tell you properly. The replay was on a lovely evening just like the first, the same crowd, the same colours: it was like a recurring dream. Except this time Porritt was wearing a blue jersey. Just to unsettle us, we thought. And the game was just like the first: us pressing, them holding on, looking for the breakaway, depending on Porritt. And Porritt was the same as ever. Yes, of course we tried out little ploys. It was as if he knew them before we did. I remember thinking: I've got to learn to *see* a game like he does. On it went, first half, second half, extra time: no score, us getting really frustrated and ragged. It was now we could have leaked in a sneak goal and lost after all that. I remember shouting, "Calm down. Don't get rattled." There was a minute to go. No penalty shoot-outs in those days. Porritt would have *loved* that. So it was our last chance. Billy Wagstaff came down the right and crossed. As usual, Porritt looked to have it covered so easily. But then Wally Ringwood pops up from nowhere and heads it in a great loop right over Porritt's arms and it makes this soft lob right to where I was waiting. For the first time we'd caught him off balance. Perfect. I remember thinking, You think you can read the game, Porritt. Well, so can I. I wasn't offside. I had an open goal. So I really cracked the ball, along the ground, straight for the corner.'

'And you scored and Winsley won,' said Jason.

'Did I heck as like,' said Grandad. 'Porritt twisted in midair like some huge panther. He made this great dive backwards. He was travelling through the air faster than the ball, I swear, and I'd hit it as hard as I knew how. And he didn't just push it away, he grabbed it, tucked it into his body, got up and cleared and trotted back as I just stood and stared at him. And he spoke to me. He said, "You can try for the rest of your life and you'll not beat me." Well, I wasn't going to be put down by him. So I answered, "As long as it takes, Porritt. As long as it takes." And just as I turned to go upfield, the final whistle blew. So I never had a chance. We shared the Cup, six months each.'

'And did you when you played against him again?'

'I never had a chance. I never saw him again.'

'Was he signed by a big club?'

'He should have been. He should have played for England. But I never heard of him again.'

Grandad looked into the fire.

'I wish I had,' he said. 'I'd love to meet him again. I've been over that shot and save every day in my mind for nearly fifty years. And it's always the same. He *still* dives and smothers the ball by the post.'

The phone rang.

'That's it,' said Grandad. 'She wants me to pick her up again. Good luck for tomorrow. I'll be there.'

The last match was at home. There was a large crowd of Winsley parents – and quite a few from Feldover. The sun shone. On a table near the halfway line was the Schools League Shield waiting to be presented. Jason and the rest felt all the butterflies before a big occasion.

Grandad was with Jason's parents. Jason couldn't stop thinking about Grandad's story. He had even dreamed about it: had seen a great lithe panther swoop on every shot he made. When he stepped out on the field his stomach turned over; Feldover wore an all green strip against Winsley's all red. Their goalkeeper came out last. Jason gasped. He pinched himself to be sure he wasn't still dreaming. He was looking at a figure very tall for his age, but not thin and lanky, in blue jersey and black shorts. Jason hadn't seen him before. Still, the first game at Feldover had been in January and half the regular players in both teams were off with 'flu.

The whistle blew. The match was on.

It didn't take long for Jason to realize they were playing a different class of team from the rest in the League. Feldover were *good*. They played neatly, for each other. For a while, their accurate passing bemused Darren, Dilip and the rest. Jason had an ugly feeling they were going to be swamped. Puggy Thorpe had to make a couple of scrambled saves before they came to terms with it and began to get a feel of the game.

At last, Jason got involved as well. Terry worked the ball out of the Winsley half. His pass found Errol who slipped it through for Jason to have his first goal attempt. He was pleased with it: the ball travelled sweetly off his boot. The big Feldover goalkeeper scooped it up as if he were playing with a toddler and cleared. Almost at once the ball came back to Jason. He shot high for the top corner. The goalkeeper reached out and caught it like someone taking a jam jar from the larder shelf.

Jason shook his head. The feeling that he was dreaming a rerun of Grandad's Minor Cup Final was something he had better get rid of.

Now Winsley pressed hard. But the Feldover defence was well drilled and knew exactly when to leave it to this big and remarkable goalkeeper. Until just before half-time. Now Jason really thought he had the goal at his mercy. He shot, was about to throw his arms up in delight – and the big blue-black figure was there from nowhere, lunging across to tip the ball away for a corner.

A shout came, clearly above the rest, from the Feldover teacher standing with Mr Jenkin.

'Well done, Porritt.'

The whistle blew. The teams trooped off. Jason had a lot to think about.

Apart from gathering that he was pleased, Jason hardly heard a word Mr Jenkin said at half-time. History really *was* repeating itself. What must Grandad be thinking?

The second half started. Like the end of the first half, like the two long-ago Cup Finals, Winsley pressed, peppered the Feldover goal. Their defence stood firm, the goalkeeper was incredible. Winsley had to watch for breakaways – but they were not going to be caught out again like they nearly were at Costers Park.

Time went on. The Winsley parents were nearly demented. Their team stayed calm. But Jason was beginning to have a nasty feeling. The outcome would be worse than for Grandad. The match would be a draw. But this time Feldover would win, just because they thrashed a few twerps last week 9–0.

A minute to go. One last assault. Dilip sent Terry away down the left. He crossed high to where Jason waited in his favourite goal-hanging spot. But what was the use? This new Porritt had it covered, would just pluck it out of the air like he had all the rest.

Then Errol popped up from nowhere. He headed it on, high in a big loop over Porritt's head, straight to Jason.

Only for the splittest of seconds did Jason see again everything that Grandad had told him. He would bring the ball down, shoot hard and low for the corner – but Porritt would twist in midair, dive across and smother the ball just by the post.

And he did. Just as agile, just as stunning, like a great panther swooping across Jason's vision. Someone else had been told the story of the Minor Cup Final.

But Jason hadn't shot. He'd drawn his foot back – and then held it. He watched till the flying body had passed him. Then he rolled the ball past the prone Porritt into the other corner of the net.

The parents went even wilder. Mr Jenkin allowed himself a smile of satisfaction. The rest of the team mobbed Jason. Porritt picked the ball out of the net and gave Jason a rueful glance.

The final whistle blew. Mr Jenkin and his Feldover colleague rushed onto the pitch to marshal their teams for the presentation.

But before he joined them, Jason ran to where he could see Grandad standing on the touchline. He had left Jason's parents and was next to a thin figure hunched in a wheelchair.

'Good lad, Jason,' said Grandad. 'I'm proud of you.'

The figure in the wheelchair held out an overcoated sleeve with a blotched, bony but still huge hand sticking out of the end. A weak voice from the depths of a flat cap and muffler spoke. 'You did well, boy. It took you long enough.' Then, to someone the other side, 'Don't

fret, lad. There'll be more games.'

Jason looked up. Porritt stood there.

Now Jason looked more carefully into the depths of the muffler. He saw a thin, sunken face, inflamed eyes. This man had been in a wheelchair for many years. Jason looked up at Grandad questioningly. Grandad nodded. There was deep sadness in his eyes.

'You'd better go and get your Shield,' he said.

As they both turned, the old Porritt reached out and grabbed Grandad's arm with his skeleton hand. Grandad put his arms round the thin shoulders protectively.

'I told you,' he said. 'As long as it takes.'

The old Porritt looked up at him, smiling slightly.

'The young ones,' he said hoarsely. 'They're all right, aren't they?'

'None better,' said Grandad.

Jason and Porritt left the two old men together and ran off to join the others.

THERE'S ONLY ONE
HARRY JACKSON!

by Dennis Whelehan

Harry and I were waiting outside the door that said
'Club Officials and Players Entrance'. It was already
quite dark. A handful of people in club shirts and woolly
hats were stamping feet and blowing through fists.

Harry broke a roll of mints and gave me half. There
was an odd one. Harry bit it carefully in two. That was
Harry all over – a stickler for fair play.

'You'll never get it,' I said, checking my watch.
'Probably he doesn't even give autographs.'

'I can try,' said Harry.

'Five more minutes,' I said, 'then I'm off.'

I wasn't mad on football. Knocking about with Harry
meant that I went to the odd game on Saturdays – that
is, when we weren't playing for one of the school teams.

I'd certainly learnt a lot in the past couple of years, because Harry was a walking encyclopaedia on football. Still, he had to put up with my mania – Hollywood Westerns.

'There he is,' said Harry.

Everybody else drew back in disappointment as a small man with greying hair came through the door. Harry poked the book and pencil under his nose.

'Can I have your autograph?'

The man looked surprised, then pleased. He grinned and signed the book. Harry gazed on the page with reverence.

'Alan Kenny,' he said. 'Now that's what I call a star.'

I was already heading for the bus stop. Harry ran to catch up with me.

'You must be the only person in the country,' I said, 'who collects the autographs of referees.'

Harry Jackson wasn't really weird. His ambition was to be a referee. Knowing him, there was every likelihood he'd achieve it. We certainly went to the right school. Ashley Manor, under its headmaster, Mr Corke, was football mad.

The Monday morning assembly consisted largely of notices about football. Mr Corke read out the results of all the house matches, and we had to clap the goal scorers.

Then he launched into his favourite topic – the rivalry with St Gabriel's. He was a tubby, bald man, and when he got excited his head shone. It was shining now.

'We have never beaten St Gabriel's,' said Mr Corke, 'never even achieved a draw. But this week it will be different.'

The whole school was silent. Nobody believed him for a minute.

On Monday evenings Harry came round to my house. He brought his football videos, but we didn't just enjoy the games. Harry kept stopping them to talk about refereeing decisions.

'The ref missed that,' said Harry, jumping up and stabbing his finger at the screen. 'Look at that player taking the throw-in. He's only got one hand on the ball.'

And Harry sat down, shaking his head at the sad state of World Cup refereeing. A few minutes later he stopped the film again.

'That defender's clearly over the ball. That's not tackling, that's kicking. I'd show the yellow card.'

I would retaliate by making him watch my favourite bits of *Gunfight at the OK Corral*.

The main reason Harry came round was to accompany my dad to evening classes in refereeing. Mr Corke had started them up to get parents involved in school games. There were so many house matches that Ozzie Osbourne, the games teacher, couldn't cope. Harry was allowed to attend the classes with Mr Corke's permission.

'I wish you could go in my place,' grumbled Dad as

he got ready to leave the warm house. He got dragged in because he was a member of the P.T.A.

'You'll never referee a game at school,' I said as Harry and Dad went out to the car. 'Ozzie would never allow it.'

Ozzie hated coaching the parents. He hated Harry, not to mention the whole of the human race.

'I might,' said Harry.

'Five pounds bet?'

'You're on,' said Harry.

Five pounds would buy the video of *Stagecoach*, the best Western ever made.

Wednesday afternoons were reserved for sport. In the football season, that meant house matches. Sensible people skipped off to the local McDonalds unless they happened to be playing, but Harry stood in the cold watching Moore House versus Greaves. (You've guessed – Mr Corke named them after famous footballers.)

'I need the experience,' Harry said. He didn't come to see the game as much as to spot the infringements. I was playing as an unenthusiastic centre back for Moore, and fifteen minutes into the first half we were trailing 2–0.

The referee was terrible. He was a parent, a graduate from Ozzie's course. One of the lads on our side, a short, ginger-haired winger called O'Connor, was really talented. He was Harry's main rival for a place in the school team against St Gabriel's.

O'Connor had a scoring chance, a lovely through ball

that came from nowhere. He ran on to it, and a Greaves defender promptly took his legs from under him.

'Foul,' shouted Harry. He had been offering advice since the kickoff, and the parent ignored him.

'Free kick,' Harry shouted again.

The parent blew his whistle, but not to award a foul. He'd had enough. He strode grimly across to Harry, expecting him to back away. Harry stood his ground.

'Are you trying to tell me my job?' demanded the parent.

'I will if you like,' said Harry. 'Your job is to protect the skilful players, and not let them get kicked out of the game.'

The parent had to make an effort not to flatten Harry there and then. And yet Harry wasn't normally cheeky. It was just that his sense of fair play trapped him into dangerous behaviour sometimes.

'I don't give up my afternoons to take lip from the likes of you,' said the parent. 'How would you like the lousy job?'

He looked around for approval, certain that he'd pushed Harry into a corner.

'Hand over the whistle,' said Harry.

The parent hesitated. Harry had called his bluff, and he really was fed up with refereeing.

'Take it,' he said, and hurried off to his car.

Harry called the two captains into the middle of the field and talked to them. We could see them nodding their heads. Then he appointed a couple of lads to act as linesmen – the parent had been managing without them. He consulted his watch and restarted the game with a dropped ball.

And it was a different game. The players behaved themselves. Harry gave an offside against Greaves House, and nobody complained. He gave a couple of free kicks for shirt tugging, and had one of them retaken because the ball wasn't stationary. O'Connor tucked away a goal before half-time.

In the second half, I tried for a penalty by rolling into the box after a robust tackle. Harry wasn't deceived – he made diving motions with his hands, and waved play on. O'Connor, who was having the game of his life, made it to the byline and crossed a ball that was caught by the wind and floated under the crossbar. It had turned into a real game.

And then everything stopped. Ozzie stormed on to the field and grabbed the whistle from Harry. The narrow eyes set in his thin face were blazing with anger. Apparently the parent had made a complaint.

'Report to Mr Corke first thing on Thursday,' said Ozzie. 'Your refereeing days are over.'

Moore House lost 5–2. I paid Harry the five pound bet from an advance in my pocket money.

I waited for Harry a few metres down the corridor from Mr Corke's office. Christmas decorations hung from the ceiling, and there was holly around the pictures of famous footballers on the walls. The interview didn't last long.

'So what happened?' I asked Harry.

'I've got to write a letter of apology to the parent.'

Just then Mr Corke came out of his office. He walked in our direction.

'Whose photo do you think he has on his desk?' Harry whispered as he approached.

'His wife? Madonna?'

'Only Nat Lofthouse, signed and dated 1958 – the year he got the winning two goals against Manchester United in the Cup Final.'

Mr Corke stopped and spoke to Harry.

'Mr Osborne tells me you're hoping to be picked for the St Gabriel's match. We need a result.'

Mr Corke often sounded like a football manager. All he needed was a cigar and a sheepskin coat.

'You might do better for us as a referee,' said Mr Corke.

'I'd still have to play by the rules,' said Harry seriously. 'The stricter the referee, the better the match.'

'Of course, of course,' said Mr Corke quickly. 'I was only joking.'

But I wasn't so sure. Mr Corke desperately wanted to beat St Gabriel's. Ozzie would be the referee, and he had better be unbiased. Playing or not, Harry would be watching. Like a hawk.

We were eating Christmas lunch when Ozzie silenced the chatter and rattle of plates to make an announcement. Mr Corke considered the interschool match to be so important that there was to be a trial game – a rehearsal, in other words – that very afternoon.

'Crazy,' said Harry. 'There's bound to be injuries. The real match is on Friday afternoon.'

Teams were quickly picked. Harry was in the School team, and I was playing for the Rest. Still, it meant missing double French – games, crosswords and film treats to mark the end of term, all more boring than ordinary lessons.

The game was refereed by Ozzie. Within five minutes he was threatening to send Harry off.

'That was a tackle from behind,' protested Harry, pulling his sock down to show stud marks on the back of his leg.

'I didn't see it,' said Ozzie.

'You would if you kept up with the game,' said Harry.

He was right. Ozzie had a bad cold, and like us he thought the trial was unnecessary. He stood around the halfway line, and didn't even bother to come up for corners.

I was playing well back. I hardly saw Harry. There was no score at half-time. It was a thoroughly rotten game.

Mr Corke appeared on the touchline for the second half.

'Come on the School,' he bawled. And then, when he thought nobody would hear, 'Get stuck in, you layabouts. Short passes. Tap and run, tap and run.'

Ozzie blew for offside, and Harry led the players who mobbed him.

'Never offside,' howled Harry. 'How could anyone interfere with play when he's flat on his back? Play the game, ref.'

Only the presence of Mr Corke kept Harry on the pitch. Otherwise it would have been quick march, and an early bath.

'Last warning,' said Ozzie menacingly.

And then the accident happened.

Harry took a free kick. The defenders for the Rest formed a wall, me among them, covering half the goal. The goalkeeper took care of the other half. All good tactics.

Harry decided to drive the ball straight through the wall. He might score, or one of the School team might pick up a ricochet. But it all went badly wrong.

Harry hit the ball really hard, and sliced it. Ozzie, who wasn't even watching, took the full force of the shot straight in the face.

There was a gasp from both teams. Ozzie spun around, covered his face with his hands and fell.

We ran to help, joined by Mr Corke. We lifted Ozzie to his feet. He was groggy, and bleeding freely from the nose. Mr Corke took him off to hospital in his car. Harry offered to referee the rest of the match, but it was disbanded.

On the way home, he was in an unsentimental mood.

'He had it coming,' he said, 'staring around, looking anywhere but at the ball.'

An unpleasant suspicion entered my mind.

'Harry,' I began, 'you didn't—'

'No, I did not,' he answered forcefully, and I knew that he was telling the truth. Somebody else might take a pot shot at Ozzie, but not Harry. It wouldn't be playing the game.

We passed the bus ride speculating about who would referee the big match if Ozzie was crocked. None of our teachers were up to it. So they would have to nominate somebody from St Gabriel's. What else could they do?

Ozzie wore a plaster across his nose on Friday morning. The area around his eyes was an interesting shade of purple, but he was sitting on stage with the rest of the staff for the final assembly of term.

'Today's the day,' said Mr Corke, 'the day we beat St Gabriel's. And we'll all be there to support our lads.'

Rain was already streaming down the windows of the hall. Ninety per cent of the school would take the afternoon off, indoors, in the warm.

'The team will be posted at break,' said Mr Corke, dismissing us.

There was little in the way of lessons on the last morning of term. Most teachers let us play games, but no gambling. (If only they knew!)

At break Harry and I ran to the notice-board. I didn't expect to be in the team. But Harry wasn't in either.

'That rotter Ozzie—'

Harry cut me off.

'He's playing O'Connor, it's an attacking side,

and that's fair enough.'

But I wasn't convinced.

We were on our way to the Carol Concert when we bumped into an excited group outside the gym. They were wearing gym kit – Ozzie never gave free periods at the end of term.

'What's up?' I asked.

'Haven't you heard the news? Ozzie's fainted. Fell off the wall bars.'

'Sorry I missed it,' I said.

Then Harry and I exchanged glances.

'So who's going to referee the match?' I said.

We found out midway through the concert. A prefect tiptoed in and pushed his way to where Harry and I were standing at the back.

'Hey, you,' he said to Harry. 'Corke wants you in his office. On the double.'

I sneaked out behind Harry. When he emerged from the office, he looked bewildered. He also looked delighted.

'I'm reffing the game.'

I could hardly believe it.

'You mean it won't be postponed?'

'It would have to be next term. Corke says nobody would be interested.'

'Nobody's interested now,' I said. 'And why doesn't he get a teacher from St Gabriel's? They must have some able-bodied staff over there.'

'Apparently not possible. They're all away for the

afternoon on National Curriculum meetings.'

We were alone in the deserted corridor. Voices singing 'Once in Royal David's City' drifted in from the hall.

'It's your big chance,' I said. 'Corke will expect you to go easy on our team.'

'I won't do that,' said Harry. 'This is one game that will get played by the rules.'

The rain had turned to sleet, and the light was poor when Ashley Manor kicked off against St Gabriel's. There were few spectators – mostly First Years, shouting to keep their spirits up.

Mr Corke stood with the headmaster of St Gabriel's under a huge, striped umbrella. They looked glum, and didn't speak.

Harry summoned the two captains to the centre circle for the tossing of the coin. He was wearing two watches, and a whistle dangled from a cord at his wrist. The match began.

Harry had an easy task. Fouls were caused by the muddy conditions rather than by intent, and nobody disputed his decisions. It had all the makings of a dull, dogged game. There was no score at half-time.

It was well into the second half before the game came alive. O'Connor picked up the ball in the midfield, beat a couple of defenders by sheer speed, and lobbed the ball across to the opposite wing.

Harry kept up with the action, running with a

stooping posture as if studying the players' feet.

The ball was returned to O'Connor. He hit it first time, a low, skidding shot that the keeper stooped to gather but couldn't hold. The greasy ball spun into the back of the net.

'Goal!' roared Mr Corke, and the striped umbrella bounced about like a giant kite. We were actually leading St Gabriel's! I checked my watch. Fifteen minutes left to play. If we could only hang on, it would be a famous victory.

What Harry needed was a nice, uneventful end to the match. But that, unfortunately, wasn't what he got.

The goal changed everything. Both teams were cold and tired, and the playing conditions were appalling. There were disputed corners, disputed throw-ins and shouts for penalties every few minutes.

Harry kept control amazingly well. He backed off from the players, making no attempt to argue. Then he gave his decision and walked off quickly, whistle in mouth. It worked, and he avoided a crisis. Until the last five minutes.

St Gabriel's were in our penalty area. Two of our defenders crashed into their striker just as he was about to shoot. They all went down together.

I saw Harry hesitate. Mr Corke was jumping and waving the striped umbrella.

'Play on,' he shouted. 'No penalty.'

It was a difficult decision, but Harry had been stand-ing very close.

Immediately he was surrounded by our players, people who only a day ago had been his own team-mates. Harry backed away, then pointed to the penalty spot.

The St Gabriel's captain placed the ball, then took five deliberate steps back. When Harry blew the whistle, he jogged up to the ball and whacked it. And missed!

The volume of noise produced by the spectators was deafening. Our team were dancing on the pitch. Mr Corke had thrown the umbrella away and was clapping his hands above his head. Surely the match was over, and we had beaten St Gabriel's.

Something was happening on the pitch. There was a crowd around Harry. He spoke to the goalkeeper, then pointed again to the penalty spot.

I realized what was going on. There is a football rule that is broken at all levels. If the goalkeeper moves before the penalty-kicker makes contact with the ball, then the penalty is retaken. It is a difficult decision for even an experienced referee to get right, and it is always unpopular. Unless the movement is exaggerated, many referees overlook it. But not Harry.

A St Gabriel's defender took the kick. He drove the ball into the bottom right-hand corner of the net. Our keeper waited, then dived the wrong way.

The teams lined up, but hardly had play started when Harry blew the final whistle.

Everybody cheered. Ashley Manor hadn't won, but we had gained a draw against St Gabriel's, our best result

ever. Mr Corke's face was a picture. He looked as if he'd just got off a runaway roller coaster.

Harry picked up the ball and began to walk off the pitch. Just then, somebody called out, 'Well played, ref! There's only one Harry Jackson!'

You can say that again, I thought.

But Harry just smiled.

STAR ON A DESERT ISLAND
by Brian Morse

Gareth had known for weeks Mr Rogers was leaving the school at Christmas. He'd just put off thinking what it would mean to him personally as school football captain.

'I suppose someone else will be running the team,' he blurted out.

'Brilliant deduction. Unless he's got a way of running you by remote control from London,' said Jonathan, a clever so-and-so Gareth suspected of mockery every time his mouth opened.

'It was in the last news-letter that he was going,' Darren chipped in. 'Suppose you chucked it in the hedge as usual.'

'Gareth can't read anyway,' a boy's voice said, he didn't catch whose.

Darren dodged out of the way. 'Wasn't me!' he protested.

'Just because he kicks round a pig's bladder filled with air,' Josie Lowndes said loudly, 'and he's got the games teacher wrapped round his little finger — thinks he's it.'

Gareth moved away. Keep out of trouble. Don't be provoked. Count to ten. All the teachers constantly told him so. Make your life easier, his mum said. (And mine, she added.) Not as if Mr Rogers was even his teacher — he taught Y3, not Y6. Just the teacher responsible for the football team.

But losing Mr Rogers was painful — almost like losing a friend and Gareth didn't have too many of those. And having been made captain of the school football XI was the best thing that had ever happened to him. First, second and third best thing. Tenth. Hundredth. OK it was because Mr Rogers had thought he wouldn't play if he wasn't captain (shows how wrong teachers can be!) and without him, the only decent player in the school, the team would fall apart. But captain was what he'd wanted to be ever since he'd turned up at his first football practice in Y5, knowing he was good but not sure the teacher would realize it. How nervous he'd been that Tuesday afternoon. He remembered it like yesterday.

Thinking back, Gareth slipped into his favourite daydream. He dummied an imaginary defender, changed balance from right foot to left, and crossed to the far side of the box. Clive Nauta, Albion captain and Gareth's hero, picked it up and shot. The crowd erupted.

'Clive and Gareth!' they chanted. 'Clive and Gareth!'

Easy!

He and Clive Nauta did a victory dance.

'Daft berk!' Josie Lowndes' voice drifted across. 'Look at him showing off.'

January chill. Mist hung and dripped in the trees ringing the pitch. Hall Green were 3–1 down and try as he might Gareth didn't seem able to influence the result. He couldn't be everywhere at once – that was the trouble. He couldn't be at the back controlling that tall forward *and* in the middle collecting the ball *and* playing up front and scoring.

He could have another try though.

Tenterfields' latest attack petered out. (Gareth had made sure of that by kicking the tall forward in the shins.) Tony was dithering with the ball just outside the area.

'Here!' Gareth shouted. 'Here! Pass!' he screamed with frustration.

When the ball didn't arrive he ran across and shouldered Tony off it. He ran the ball past the tall boy, who was limping, past another of their forwards and towards a ruck of Tenterfields players huddled together in the middle of the pitch. Without conviction they advanced on him: they'd seen what he'd done to their teammate.

On the right a voice – John Francis' – shouted, 'Gareth! Here!' but Gareth didn't pass. John Francis would try something clever and lose the ball. He ploughed on and emerged on the other side of the Tenterfields players, still with the ball.

He walked it a few more yards, side-stepped the goalie and prepared to belt the ball home. *Easy!* At which point John Francis called '*Gareth! Mind!*' and a whirlwind hit him. The forward he'd fouled picked the ball off his toes and kicked it away to safety.

The whistle went. 3–1. Gareth headed off the pitch. That was the fifth game they'd lost since September. Four won, two drawn, five lost. A lousy record. He deserved better.

John Francis came after him. John Francis was a slight boy, good at his school work, well behaved, well liked by teachers – almost everything Gareth was not. For once he was in a temper. 'You're so selfish! If you'd passed it—'

'Get lost!' Gareth said.

'I warned you,' John Francis stormed. 'I was clear. I could have taken it down the wing and passed it back!'

'Didn't you hear me?' Gareth said.

Someone was shouting. 'Hall Green. Over here a minute. *Hall Green!*' Gareth and John Francis stopped.

'It's that new teacher,' John Francis said. 'The one taking Mr Rogers' class. She was watching from half-time. What's she want?'

'*Everyone here!*' she shouted. 'You two as well!'

Curious, the team gathered round her. 'I won't keep you long,' she said. Her name was Miss Evans. She and Gareth had already met in the corridor on several occasions. They'd not got on. 'I'm sorry you lost.'

'Like always, Miss!' Colin the goalkeeper said cheerfully.

'That so? Why?'

'We haven't many good players, Miss,' Colin giggled.

Speak for yourself, Gareth thought. What's she want?

'There were several excellent moves,' Miss Evans said. She looked round. She was shorter than the tallest of them, Danny. Her eyes reached Gareth and passed over him.

'Yes, you,' the teacher said. She was smiling at John Francis. 'You made a couple of really nice runs. If you'd got the ball at the end you might have made it three-two.' She looked round the group again. Her eyes ran straight past Gareth once more. 'Tuesday nights, isn't it, your practice?'

What's that to you? Gareth thought.

'Gareth scored our goal, Miss,' Danny said loyally.

'Gareth. Oh yes. The captain.' Her eyes rested on Gareth at last. So she did know his name. 'I'm told you're quite talented,' she said. 'Have to learn to pass though, won't you? No more hogging it. And no more nicking the ball off your own side.'

'Me, Miss?'

Gareth made his empty-handed-down-to-knees ape gesture.

The team laughed.

'If I'd been reffing you'd have been off straightaway for the way you kicked that Tenterfields forward.'

'Me, Miss?'

'Maybe we could get together some dinner-time,' Miss Evans said briskly. 'Talk tactics. Set targets. You need to get sorted out.' The mist began to drizzle drops of rain. 'I'll send a note round.'

The penny dropped at last.

This woman was taking Mr Rogers' place.

'Nice runs!' Gareth mocked John Francis.

'At least I *think* when I play!' John Francis retorted.

At least Mr Rogers had passed on his name. What had he told her? 'Quite talented.' *Quite*, not *very*. All her praise had been for John Francis. Gareth wasn't used to that kind of treatment. Was that really all Mr Rogers had told her – 'quite talented'?

'Everyone's on trial,' Miss Evans said. 'Next game we'll keep Mr Rogers' line-up – no reason to change it till I know you better. But a couple of Y5 players look really promising – I took them for games yesterday. They're coming to the practice. So everything's up for grabs.'

Gareth forced himself to speak. 'And me, Miss. Am I still captain?' Nothing had been said or hinted at.

'Glad you've mentioned that. *I said* – everything's up for grabs, captaincy included.'

Colin asked some stupid question, Tony another. Gareth made for the door. She wouldn't choose him – that was obvious. No way he'd play under someone else.

'Where do you think you're going?' the voice came – as Gareth knew it would.

'Toilet, Miss.'

'You're a big boy. Big boys can wait.'

'I'm desperate, Miss.' As soon as he said it Gareth knew he'd made a mistake.

'We don't want any accidents, then, do we? Off you go.'

One or two of the team tittered.

'Gareth,' Miss Evans said as he opened the door. 'You don't have a problem with me, do you?'

'How do you mean, Miss?'

'Because I'm a woman. You know – women don't know anything about football, that kind of thing.'

'No, Sir – I mean, Miss!'

The team roared.

'One–all – maybe,' Miss Evans said.

Even though he was trying to keep out of trouble, the fight began as they were coming in after dinner. 6W and 6L walked in from the playground in parallel lines. A hand came snaking over and caught Gareth on the back of the neck. Josie Lowndes' twin brother, Richard. Gareth knew it without looking. He was meant to know who it was. Richard had been niggling him all dinner-time.

As they came in through the swing doors Gareth thumped Richard. Trust Josie to join in. She was a big girl and liked scraps more than most boys. Gareth felt absolutely no shame in thumping her back.

'Fight! Fight!'

A dinner lady tried to separate them and failed.

John Francis grabbed his right arm and hung on. 'Don't be an idiot!' he shouted. 'They want you in trouble!'

'Butt out, dummy!' Gareth threw him off. He bounced off Josie.

Mrs Wass, 6W's class teacher, arrived.

'All muscle and no sense,' she breathed in his face. 'The class and school bully and an idiot into the bargain. I'm having a word with Miss Evans about your footballing activities.'

'I'm not a bully, Miss!' Gareth said, stung with indignation.

From behind the teacher Richard winked at him. Stitched up.

'What you sticking up for him for?' Josie said to John Francis indignantly.

'I've no idea,' he said. He rubbed his nose which had banged into Josie's shoulder.

Saturday morning. Since his agreed punishment (convenient for Miss Evans) was to lose the captaincy (she'd given it to John Francis) Gareth had been very tempted not to turn up. To his own surprise, almost, he was at school at ten to ten, one of the first.

'Glad to see you, Gareth,' Miss Evans said.

'Hi!' John Francis said sheepishly. Gareth ignored them both.

The other team members avoided his eye. Everyone

in the team, everyone in Y6 knew how much the captaincy had meant to him.

'Pass pass pass!' Miss Evans said when they were changed. 'The new players—' it had been her lucky day: a couple of Y6s with 'flu had allowed her to bring the Y5s in – 'I want them fully included. This is a team game, remember. No use being brilliant on your own. No earthly use being a star on a desert island. OK, let's get stuck in and win!'

'Where do you want us to play?' Jason, one of the Y5s, asked Gareth.

'You ask *me* that!' John Francis said sharply.

The match started well enough. Ten minutes gone John Francis pushed the ball across the St Martin's defence and Gareth coming in from the right had little else to do but thunder it past the goalie.

At half-time 1–0.

A minute into the second half St Martin's scored an equalizer. Five minutes later they were 2–1 ahead, both goals Jason's fault.

'Whose stupid idea was it to play him?' Gareth stormed as they ran back the second time. He said it loudly for Miss Evans's benefit, but she was talking intently to a man who'd just appeared on the line.

'Stay on the right,' John Francis said, 'the way we planned. You're trying to be everywhere again, like Miss said you shouldn't.'

'*Miss! Her!* What does she know about football?'

'A lot more than Mr Rogers did! Haven't you noticed?'

As Gareth's fists went up only the ref, a St Martin's teacher, saved John Francis. 'This is a game of football,' he said. 'Keep your personal differences for off the field.'

'The players opposite you are totally useless,' John Francis said. 'If we keep feeding the ball out to you—'

'And those useless objects behind us?'

'I'll worry about them,' John Francis said.

Gareth looked towards the line. Miss Evans and the man she was with were watching him. The man was in a smart suit with an expensive overcoat unbuttoned at the front. Surely he recognized him from somewhere?

Gareth looked back at John Francis. What he'd said about Mr Rogers was still smarting. John Francis stood his ground. 'Well?' he said. For a second Gareth almost admired him. There weren't many brave enough to cross him except lunatics like the Lowndes twins.

'Come on, Gareth! Show them what you're made of!' Miss Evans shouted.

Gareth saluted John Francis. 'OK, cap'n!' he said.

Five minutes later Jason picked apart the St Martin's attack and sent a long ball over Gareth's head. John Francis was perfectly right. The St Martin's players on that side were useless. Gareth collected the ball, cut in from the line and angled it between the post and the goalkeeper's body. *Easy!* Worthy of his hero Clive Nauta!

Clive and Gareth! Clive and Gareth! Gareth whooped his way back to the restart.

'Well done, Gareth! Brilliant!' Miss Evans shouted. She turned and smiled at the man. Gareth was sure he recognized him from somewhere.

3–2. Gareth made off home without changing. He might have scored two – and made the third – but Miss Evans had been full of how brilliantly the two new players had done (with a rap over the knuckles for Jason's mistakes after half-time), of how people had done their best to stay in position, how well John Francis had 'marshalled his troops' (whatever that meant). Hardly a word of praise for him. Without him they'd have scored nothing, they'd have been destroyed. Finally nothing about him getting the captaincy back.

He slipped between the mobile classrooms. The back entrance to the school was padlocked at weekends but there was a fence you could climb.

Gareth didn't notice Miss Evans and the man chatting till too late.

'Where are you going?' Miss Evans called as Gareth tried to draw back. 'I might be new here but I know this way's out of bounds.'

'Miss—'

'Well?'

The man – Gareth stared. Close to, Gareth was even more sure he recognized him.

'Well off you go, then, the proper way.'

'Miss—' he blurted it out. 'Next game – who's going to be captain?'

'Captain?' From the look on her face he could tell straightaway it wasn't going to be him.

'It doesn't matter.' Gareth wished himself a million miles away. He turned.

'Great game, Gareth,' the man said, smiling. 'There's something I wanted—'

'Who cares!' Gareth said. He walked past them, made for the fence and climbed over.

When he was walking down the main road he realized who the man was.

The footballers were gathered in a noisy bunch in the middle of the playground before start of school Monday morning, Jason and the other Y5 among them. Gareth had been smarting all weekend. He was still smarting. He swerved to one side.

'Hey, Gareth!' Colin called. 'Where are you off to? Come here!'

Gareth stopped. 'What for?'

'That man with Miss Evans at the game – you remember?'

'What about him?'

'That was Clive Nauta, the Albion captain. Tony's dad recognized him.'

'Of course I knew it was him,' Gareth said. 'Why do you think I was extra brilliant Saturday?'

Not often you spit in the face of your hero, Gareth thought. How'd he been supposed to recognize him out of his football gear, especially as he'd only ever seen him in photographs?

Jason followed him into the out-of-bounds cloakroom.

'That second goal you scored Saturday was ace. My dad said—'

'I couldn't care less what your dad says.' Stupid little kids, sucking up to Y6s. Who wanted them? No-one. Gareth turned his back.

The moment later Gareth regretted what he'd said. Wasn't he an expert on hero worship? He turned but Jason had gone.

'I've two things to say,' Miss Evans said to Gareth. 'Do you want the good first or the bad?' When he didn't reply she said, 'The bad, from your point of view, is that John Francis stays captain. The team, especially you, did much better playing under him. Why you find being captain so important I do not know.' She paused. Ask your boyfriend, Gareth thought murderously. 'The good is I'll forget your disobedience Saturday morning. But just be warned – I won't ignore anything like it again.'

'Yes, Miss.'

'Off you go' Miss Evans said. 'Oh by the way,' she said to his back, 'Clive Nauta – you've probably heard of him? All he wanted was to invite you along to the junior training sessions he's going to run at the Albion ground at half-term. He thought you had potential. A shame you didn't care.'

*

The next game, a rearranged fixture, was in school time. Y6 was coming to watch the last thirty minutes. As the two classes arrived at half-time the score was one–all.

'Not quite Wembley,' Miss Evans said as the team gathered round her before the restart, 'but almost as nerve-racking. Ignore them and play your usual game.'

Gareth did feel nervous playing in front of all Y6. 'I'll trip you if you come near me,' Richard Lowndes had promised at dinner-time. 'I mean it.'

Mrs Wass lined up 6W. You could hear her issuing death threats about behaviour.

Miss Evans said quietly, 'You remember that move we practised – John Francis setting off on a dummy run across the box and Tony pushing the ball across to Gareth? I think it might be the time to try it.'

'OK, Miss,' John Francis said.

The whistle went.

'No Clive Nauta today, Miss?' Colin asked.

'No, Albion are away in London tonight. Why?'

'Nothing, Miss.' Colin grinned round the group.

Gareth dropped his eyes. The last thing he wanted was mention of Clive Nauta. Miss Evans hadn't said whether, despite his rudeness, the invitation to the Albion still stood. Gareth couldn't bring himself to ask.

'He's not my boyfriend,' Miss Evans said, 'if that's what everyone's thinking. He's my brother-in-law.'

'Who's your boyfriend then, Miss?' Colin asked cheekily.

'Bobby Charlton,' she said.

'Is he famous too, Miss?' Colin asked.

'Look him up in an encyclopaedia!' Miss Evans laughed. 'Right, go away and play.'

Ten minutes to go the score was still one-all.

'Tony?' John Francis called. 'Gareth? What about it?'

They nodded.

The opportunity came almost immediately.

As one of the full-backs came out to challenge him John Francis laid the ball back to Tony then began to run across the box as if he expected Tony to pass it back to him. The second full-back followed him. The first went out to challenge Tony. Tony held the ball just long enough to allow Gareth to run in from the right. The pass was near perfect.

He and Tony whooped their way back to the centre circle.

John Francis clapped his hands. 'Only a few minutes to go. Don't let's give it away.'

The ref was looking at his watch when Jason broke up an opposition attack. 'This way! This way!' Gareth waved and shouted but instead Jason deliberately pushed the ball up the left. The other Y5, Hardip, collected it and ran the ball up the line. Gareth kept pace with him on the far side.

'Come on, give it to Gareth!' Mrs Wass screamed. A piece of mud hit Gareth in the back of his neck. 'Richard Lowndes! Come here!' Mrs Wass bellowed. '*Come here!*'

118

Hardip got tangled with two defenders, stumbled through them and managed to boot the ball into the centre before falling over. Gareth set off to retrieve it.

When he had it under control the defenders were back in position. He looked around. John Francis was on Gareth's right but blocked.

'On your left! Jason!' John Francis urged.

Gareth glanced left to where Jason was clear, Jason who was hardly speaking to him, Jason who in revenge had been feeding the ball up the left instead of the right all afternoon. Then Gareth saw a way through the defence for himself. He could already see the way he'd side-step them.

'Let Jason have it!' John Francis insisted. 'Gareth!'

Gareth had only a fraction of a second to decide.

'Very unselfish of you, Gareth,' Miss Evans said as they walked back into school. 'I thought for a moment you were going it on your own. I wouldn't have blamed you.'

'Jason was better placed,' John Francis said seriously.

'Just following orders,' Gareth said.

Mr Rogers would never have seen I had a choice to make, he thought.

'You made Jason very happy,' Miss Evans said. 'Just look at him.'

'He's showing off, Miss,' John Francis said disapprovingly.

'I told you he'd be good, didn't I?' Miss Evans said.

'Gareth? Admit it!'

'He is good,' Gareth said. 'But, Miss—'

'Yes?'

Their eyes met.

'There was something I wanted to ask you, Miss.'

'What about? The captaincy?'

'No, Miss.' He'd forgotten that. 'You know what you were saying. About the Albion.'

'The training sessions? Clive Nauta? Well—' Miss Evans said.

Gareth waited his fate.

DANIEL SAVES THE DAY?
by Elizabeth Dale

The ball was perfect. It came high over everyone's heads and landed three metres ahead of her. Lizzie chased after it, dodged past one defender, put the ball through the legs of another, and raced towards the open goal. Everyone was cheering. She drew back her foot, whacked the ball and it went flying . . . over the cross-bar.

'No!' Lizzie sat up with a start, panting. She stared all around her and then flopped back on the bed. It was only a dream! What a relief! She closed her eyes. So, if it was only a dream, why did she have such a bad feeling? What was the matter? Everything was going to be fine, at least it would be if she could get back to sleep. The last thing Highway Middle needed was a captain who was too tired to run, let alone think.

She tossed and turned all night. Every time she went to sleep, it seemed she had some kind of football nightmare, missing goals, falling over, making a fool of herself. In one she was playing with a ball that was made of red jelly. Everyone else could kick it all right, but every time she tried, it stuck to her foot!

'You look pale!' said her mum, the next morning. 'Don't tell me you're nervous!'

'What?! Nervous about a silly girls' match?' cried Daniel, her brother. 'It'll be a doddle. The other team will be too busy trying not to get their shorts dirty and making sure their hair still looks nice. They won't notice what you're doing!'

'Daniel!' cried Mum. 'Don't be so horrible! It's going to be a tough match.' She turned back to Lizzie. 'Although I'm sure Lizzie will be able to cope . . . you've won plenty of tough matches before, haven't you?'

Lizzie pulled a face. 'This one's different,' she said. 'I'm captain, it's my team, and it's the first round of the Cup. We might get knocked out!'

'You'll be fine,' said her mum, encouragingly.

'Yeah!' smiled Lizzie. If only! If everything was going to be fine, why did she still have this terrible fear that something was going to go wrong?

Everyone else at school had bags of confidence. Somehow that made everything worse.

'I was so excited, I could hardly eat my breakfast!' said Carly. 'I've got this pain . . .'

'Just think, our first ever real match!' cried Trisha.

'What if we lose?' muttered Lizzie.

'Lose?!' cried Carly and Trisha together, as though the idea had never occurred to them.

'Not with you as captain!' said Jenny.

'We could . . . easily,' said Lizzie. 'We've never played an all-girls' team before. We don't know what we're up against.'

'Listen, Lizzie, if you can win the Cup playing in the boys' league, you can certainly beat an all-girls' team.'

'Why? Because girls aren't as good as boys?!'

'No,' said Carly, uncertainly. 'Of course not. We're just as good as the boys.'

'Better!' said Trisha.

'Yes,' said Jenny.

'Well, then, we'll have to play better today than we've ever played before, won't we?' said Lizzie. 'We'll have a practice at lunch-time – pass the word.'

As she ran onto the pitch at lunch-time, Lizzie started to relax. Playing football was the only time she felt happy, truly happy. It *was* going to be all right. They had a good team, they were in a winning mood. Especially her. Nothing geared her up to playing well more than being told she couldn't play. Like the council had told her last term.

'No girls in boys' teams!' they'd declared. They'd not even bothered to give a reason. Not a real reason. They'd said it wasn't fair to girls to play with boys, so they'd barred them altogether. As if that was fair! There had been only one thing left for Lizzie to do – form a girls' team. Everyone was really keen and the team was going to be good – one day. But Mr Jenks had entered them in the Sussex Girls' League and now they had been given their first match – in the Cup. Everything hinged on today.

She passed to Trisha, who turned and volleyed it towards the top left-hand corner. But Kate saved it. Good old Kate, who had arms so long you felt she could almost reach from one side of the goal to the other.

Yes, everything was going to be all right . . . wasn't it? So why did she still have this awful, nagging fear?

Lizzie couldn't concentrate on afternoon lessons. They should be relaxing now, heading to their match. The boys would be if they had a Cup match. But there were so few girls' teams, not only did they have to travel twenty miles to get to a match, they had to do it after three o'clock – following an afternoon of maths!

'I feel awful,' Carly whispered to her.

'Don't worry!' said Lizzie. 'You'll be all right, once we start playing.'

Finally, the bell rang. As Lizzie and her friends rushed to the door, they almost cannoned into Mr Jenks. He looked terrible.

'Ah, girls,' he said. 'Look, I'm very sorry . . .'

'What?' asked Lizzie.

'I can't take you to your match this afternoon. My

neighbour's just rung. The oak tree in my garden has fallen down, crashing into my house. There's a terrible mess.'

Everyone stared at him in horror. Lizzie felt terrible. She'd *known* something was going to go wrong. Some consolation to know she was right!

'Miss Jones has very kindly agreed to take my place,' Mr Jenks continued. 'But there's one big problem. She can't drive. We need to find someone who can drive the school minibus.'

'My dad could!' said Jenny.

'Great!' said Mr Jenks.

'But he works until six.'

Everyone groaned.

'Maybe we can get one of the other teachers?' asked Jenny.

Mr Jenks shook his head. 'I've asked them all. At this short notice, no-one qualified to drive the minibus can manage it.'

'Lizzie! Thank goodness I've caught you. You forgot your lucky mascot!'

Lizzie turned. It was Daniel and Mum. Mum who drove the Cubs all over the county in their minibus.

'Mum!' cried Lizzie, taking her cuddly toy black cat. 'You're a life-saver!'

'Don't be silly, dear,' said her mum. 'I was coming in anyway to collect Daniel.'

Lizzie grinned. 'I didn't mean that!' she said. 'You can help us win the Cup!'

'Hardly!'

'You can! Will you drive us to the match tonight? Please?!' She turned to Mr Jenks. 'My mum's an expert minibus driver. She even passed a special driving test for the Cubs.'

Mr Jenks smiled at her. 'Is this true?' he asked.

Lizzie's mum nodded her head.

'I'd be very grateful if you could help us out,' said Mr Jenks. 'No-one else can drive it, so the girls can't get to their match.'

'Please?!' begged the rest of the team.

'Um, er, I don't know,' said Lizzie's mum. 'I've got Daniel, he's supposed to be having his hair cut now. What can I do with him?'

'Take me home,' said Daniel.

'Come on, Daniel!' cried Lizzie. 'Come and support us!'

'Yes!' said Jenny. 'You can be our cheerleader.'

'We'll get some pom poms out of the cupboard for you,' said Trisha. 'After all, girls cheer on boys' teams.'

'No way!' cried Daniel. 'There is no way I'm travelling in a minibus full of giggly girls!'

'Right!' said Miss Jones. 'Everyone strapped in?'

'Yes!' cried Lizzie's friends.

'Worse luck!' said Daniel.

'Let's go then!' said Lizzie's mum, turning on the engine.

Lizzie smiled at Carly, who still looked worried. To cheer her up, they sang songs all the way, wonderful, inspiring songs. All except Daniel, who sat in the corner with his personal stereo plugged into his ears and Carly, who sat there looking pale.

'Here we are!' called Lizzie's mum, finally swinging the minibus into Ramsden School driveway.

'It's going to be all right, Carly!' said Lizzie. 'We've had our disaster, we're going to be fine, now.'

Carly clutched her tummy. 'I still don't feel well,' she said.

'It's just nerves,' said Jenny.

'No it isn't, I didn't feel well last night or this afternoon. I've got a terrible tummy-ache.'

'Dear me!' said Miss Jones, feeling her forehead. 'You've got a temperature. There's no way you can play football today!'

'But she has to!' said Lizzie. 'If she doesn't, the game's off.'

'Nonsense!' said Lizzie's mum. 'You'll just have to play with ten. I bet you'll still win.'

'We can't!' said Miss Jones. 'It's not allowed.' She reached in her bag and pulled out the Cup rules. '*All teams must consist of eleven players,*' she read.

'I . . . I'm sorry,' said Carly, looking worse than ever.

'It's OK, Carly,' said Lizzie. 'We can sort this out, we must do. We can't be out of the Cup before we've even started.'

'Perhaps Ramsden will lend us a player?' suggested Trisha.

'Oh yes? Would you help another school beat your

team in the Cup? It would be like playing against a team of twelve! We have to find someone else.'

'Well, I'm sorry,' said Lizzie's mum. 'But don't look at me. There's no way I'm putting on a tiny pair of shorts and running up and down a football pitch! I'd look like a demented hippo!'

'You can't, anyway,' said Lizzie. 'You're too old.'

Suddenly Kate smiled. 'Daniel isn't too old,' she said.

'Hey!' cried Lizzie. 'Yes!'

'But he's a boy, it wouldn't be allowed,' said Lizzie's mum.

'Not if he pretends to be a girl,' said Lizzie. 'No-one but us need know.'

'But . . . a boy in our team . . . would it be fair?' asked Jenny.

Everyone frowned.

'We don't want to win the Cup by cheating,' said Trisha.

'Hold on!' said Lizzie. 'Who's cheating? For years we've been saying girls are just as good as boys at football, that we should play together. And now you're saying what? We can't have a boy in our team because boys are better than girls?'

'No,' said Trisha, slowly.

'But Ramsden might think they are,' said Kate. 'If they ever found out . . .'

'They won't!' said Lizzie. 'Anyway, Daniel is two years younger than us, so no-one can really say we're cheating.'

Everyone looked at each other uncertainly.

'Look, we wanted equality,' said Lizzie. 'It's time we let boys have some too!' She looked at Daniel. 'Whether they want to have it or not!'

Everyone laughed. Daniel was sitting there, swaying in time to his music, totally oblivious to what was being decided about him. And then he noticed everyone staring at him. He took off his headphones.

'You'll play for us, won't you, Daniel?' asked Lizzie.

'What?'

'We need you to play in our team now; Carly's ill.'

Daniel almost had a fit. 'No way!' he cried.

'Please?' asked Jenny. 'You love football! Here's your chance to play in a Cup match and be a hero.'

'You must be joking,' laughed Daniel. 'Play with girls? Me? It's degrading!'

'Boys used to play with me,' said Lizzie. 'They were glad to have me in their team.'

'But this is different,' said Daniel. 'It's a soppy girls' team! For girls! I can't play in it!'

'Yes you can. You look like a girl.'

Daniel went purple. 'Me! A girl! You're . . . you're crazy! All of you!'

'You do! What a good job you didn't have your hair cut!' said Lizzie. 'If we comb it forward . . .'

'Stop it!' said Daniel, pushing Lizzie's hands away. 'There's no way I'm playing with a load of sissy girls.'

'Please?!' begged Kate.

'What do you want? I'll give you anything you want!' said Lizzie. 'My Michael Jackson tapes, anything . . .'

'Lizzie, that's bribery!' said her mum. She turned to her son. 'Daniel, if you don't play, the team will be out of the Cup.'

'I don't care!' said Daniel. 'It's only a girls' Cup. Not worth winning.'

Lizzie folded her arms. 'Well, then,' she said, smiling. 'I'll just have to tell Susie Ollorenshaw the truth . . .'

Daniel went red. 'What do you mean?' he asked.

'Yes!' said everyone else, sensing a juicy bit of gossip and leaning forward. 'What *do* you mean? Tell us!'

'Well,' said Lizzie, 'I was just looking for my ruler in Daniel's school bag, when what should I find, but . . .'

'Stop!' cried Daniel. 'I'll do it!'

'What?'

'I'll . . . I'll play in the team.'

'And pretend to be a girl?'

'Yes,' said Daniel. 'Provided you promise not to tell anyone, *anyone*, what you found in my bag. Especially Susie Ollorenshaw.'

'Oh?!' said Jenny, desperate to know the worst.

'Jenny!' said Trisha, nudging her.

'It's a deal,' said Lizzie, grabbing his hand and shaking it before he could change his mind.

'Hooray!' cried Trisha.

'You're magic!' yelled Kate.

Daniel struggled to emerge from a welter of un-expected hugs.

'There's one more condition!' he cried, standing up.

'No-one is to hug me or kiss me. Never. Not even if I score a goal! Not even if I score ten! No-one! Got it?'

Everyone looked at each other and laughed. It was a deal!

'Right,' said Miss Jones. 'We'd better make this convincing. It's a good job a lot of you girls wear trousers to school these days and half of you are wearing Doc Martens as well, so Daniel's shoes don't look odd. But even so, we need to make him look more like a girl. What do you think, Daniel? Come here a minute.'

Daniel complained and everyone else giggled as Miss Jones brushed his hair forward.

'Mmm,' she said. 'Not quite girly enough yet. Anyone got any ideas?'

'Pierce his ears!' cried Lizzie. 'He can wear mum's earrings.'

'Spray him with perfume!' said Kate.

Miss Jones shook her head.

'He could wear my hair band,' said Carly, quietly.

'Brilliant!' said Miss Jones. Carly's hair band was sparkly and pink. As she put it in Daniel's hair, it transformed him. No-one would think he was a boy now!

'Here, wear my pretty locket,' said Lizzie, taking it off.

'And my friendship bracelet,' said Kate, thrusting it on his wrist.

'I feel a right nerd,' scowled Daniel. 'Where's a mirror?'

'No time for that,' said Miss Jones. 'Time to get changed. I'll take Carly to the sick bay. Daniel, make

131

sure you walk like a girl, shorter steps, no pushing!'

Everyone got out of the minibus, just as the other team walked round the corner, already in their kit. They all looked bigger and full of confidence. One girl walked up to Lizzie.

'Hi!' she said. 'I'm Helen, captain of Ramsden. We've met before, I used to play in our boys' team.'

'Oh, yes, hi!' said Lizzie.

'Listen,' said Helen, 'didn't you have a dishy younger brother who used to cheer your boys' team on?'

'Gulp!' went Daniel.

'Er . . .' said Lizzie, going pale.

'He's so cute! Brought him this time, have you?'

'No.' 'He's at home.' 'She hasn't got a brother,' said Lizzie, Kate and Jenny, all together.

Meanwhile, Daniel had almost climbed back in the minibus! But a big girl stopped him.

'What's the matter? Not scared, are you?' she asked.

'Er, no,' said Daniel, in a high-pitched voice.

'What do they call you?' she asked. 'Titch?!'

Daniel looked as though he was going to respond in his typical genteel boyish way – with a quick kick on the shins.

'Come on, let's get changed!' said Lizzie and Trisha, rushing up and taking one arm each as they led him inside. Daniel tried to dash in the boys' toilet with his kit, but Lizzie barred the way.

'Wrong one!' she said. 'I should try the Girls' if I were you.'

At the very thought, Daniel went pale and decided that maybe the changing room would be good enough for him. As soon as he'd hurriedly pulled on his gear, he felt a lot better. He even got quite keen.

'This is going to be fun!' he told everyone as they walked out onto the field. 'Am I going to teach you girls how to play football! Just stand back and let me score all the goals. Lizzie make sure you feed me good balls, OK? I can't do everything myself.'

'No way! Just stay in defence and keep your hair band on,' said Lizzie. 'I'm captain, remember?'

The match was hard. Ramsden were used to playing together and they were a good team. But they didn't want to win as much as Highway Middle. Unfortunately, it seemed as though half of Ramsden had stayed behind to cheer them on, whereas Highway Middle had only got Lizzie's mum.

'Come on Highway!' she cried from the sideline, waving her red scarf and jumping up and down with excitement. 'You can do it!'

Could they? Ramsden seemed to have all the play; they passed and ran off the ball with loads of confidence, whereas Highway Middle seemed to keep giving the ball away. And every time Daniel was in possession, instead of passing it, he started showing off. He tried all sorts of tricks, and seemed most of the time to be daring the opposition to take the ball off him – which they usually did. But the rest of the team managed to make up for him.

133

Finally, Highway Middle got a corner. Trisha went over to take it, signalling to Lizzie that it was going to be a far-post curler. Lizzie took up position. Trisha hit the ball perfectly and it came flying over. The opposition goalkeeper was out of position. Lizzie leapt and headed . . . but it ballooned high over the bar.

Everyone on the touchline cheered. Lizzie wanted to die. She'd never missed an open goal like that before. Never. As she picked herself up, Trisha and Jenny looked at her in stunned surprise. She shook her head. This was no good . . . especially as the ball was already in the other half of the field. Lizzie chased back, but she was too late. Ramsden's striker beat one defender, slipped past Kate, and stroked the ball into the back of the net. They'd scored!

Lizzie felt sick. She felt as if it was all her fault. As she stood waiting to kick off, she knew it was up to her as captain to get her team believing in themselves again. And then she thought . . . Ramsden's right back was a bit slow on the turn, whereas they had Trisha out on the wing – Trisha who could run like the wind.

'Down the right!' she told Jenny. The whistle blew and Lizzie passed it to Jenny, who took it forward. She slipped past one opponent and played it out to Trisha. Trisha took it into the corner, turned and chipped the ball back to Lizzie, just as they'd practised. Unfortunately, Daniel got in the way. Daniel who was supposed to be playing in defence! Lizzie called for him to pass, but he ignored her and started showing off again, side-stepping one defender, turning, twisting and finally shooting. It was going wide, but a Ramsden defender stuck out a foot anyway and deflected it to Trisha, who hammered it. And it went in! They'd equalized!

'Brilliant!' cried Lizzie, slapping her on the back.

'Well done!' smiled Daniel. 'Didn't I set it up well?'

'You're supposed to be in defence!' hissed Lizzie. 'Part of a team!'

Daniel pulled a face. 'I just wanted to score a goal,' he said.

Lizzie glared at him. Brothers!

The game seemed easier in the second half. The wind was behind them and they had the slope in their favour now. Then, after about ten minutes, Trisha was racing down the wing, with Lizzie keeping up, inside and slightly behind, ready for the pass. There was no-one except the goalie between her and the goal. Lizzie suddenly knew she was going to score. Trisha put in a perfect cross, Lizzie put on a spurt, keeping her eyes on the ball. Out of the corner of her eye she saw the goalie advancing . . . then there was a crack, and the next thing Lizzie knew, she was flat on her back in the mud.

'Foul!' cried Daniel, who was just behind.

Slowly Lizzie sat up. Her nose felt as though someone had pushed it inside her face, her whole face ached, and blood was pouring from somewhere.

'Are you all right?' asked Daniel, looking at her anxiously.

'Uh . . . er . . .' said Lizzie, touching her nose gingerly.

The referee came running over to Lizzie. 'Are you OK?' she asked. 'Do you want to go off?'

Lizzie shook her head. As she did, blood spattered across the grass.

'Are you sure? Anyway, goal kick. Seems like you were both too keen to go for the ball. It was a nasty accident.'

'Accident!' cried Daniel. 'That was no accident! The goalie made no attempt to go for the ball, she just punched Lizzie in the face! I saw, I was right here! It should be a penalty!'

The referee shook her head. 'I wasn't that far away,' she said, walking away. 'Looked like an accident to me.'

'It wasn't!' cried Daniel. 'If you think . . .'

'Stop it!' said Lizzie, grabbing her brother's leg as he went to run after her. 'You're only making things worse.'

'But she punched you . . . you look terrible . . .'

'Well, I certainly won't feel any better if you get yourself sent off!' said Lizzie. 'I need you, we've got a match to win! Help me up!'

'I'm OK!' she added as the rest of the team gathered round. 'Come on, let's show them how tough we are! Trisha, that was a brilliant pass, just do it again!'

Trisha grinned. 'I'd do it ten times,' she said, 'if a certain person would give me the ball!' She looked at Daniel.

'Don't worry!' he said. 'I won't let you down!'

And he didn't. Anger had transformed Daniel. Instead of messing around, hogging the ball, he started playing like a member of the team. He ran hard, chased every ball, and when he won it, he did something useful with it. Three times Highway Middle came close to scoring, but three times they were denied. It seemed as if the ball would never go in the net! And all the time, the minutes were ticking away. Highway threw everything into attack, desperate to win. Daniel spent hardly any time in his own half. Instead he was up in attack, supporting his team, trying to kill every move by the other side before it had even begun. But that left them open to break-aways. Several times he and Jenny had to race back to stop Ramsden, and once it was only a magnificent save from Kate that prevented them going behind once more.

Lizzie's mum could hardly stand the suspense. 'Come on Highway!' she croaked, as Kate took a goal kick. She thumped it long and hard upfield. A Ramsden defender trapped the ball, but Daniel dispossessed her and passed to Lizzie. She controlled it, and headed straight for the Ramsden goal. There was no-one inside to pass it to. She slowed down and turned, wondering whether to pass it back to Daniel.

'Shoot!' he cried, as the defence turned towards him.

'Come on, Lizzie!' yelled her mum. Lizzie looked at the ball, shimmied to the left and hammered the ball. The Ramsden goalie leapt, despairingly got her fingertips to the ball, but she couldn't stop it. The net billowed as the ball hit it . . .

'Hooray!' cried Daniel.

'Brilliant!' yelled Trisha and Jenny, thumping Lizzie on the back.

Lizzie punched the air with delight. If they could just hold on, they'd won . . .

'Everyone back!' she told her team. 'They're going to throw everything at us now!'

But Ramsden seemed to sense defeat. They kept hitting long balls hopefully towards the Highway goal, aiming at anyone, and Highway just kept thumping it back at them. The game seemed to be lasting forever . . . but then the final whistle went at last! They'd won!

'We did it!' cried Lizzie, jumping up and down.

'Fantastic!' shouted Trisha.

'Wonderful! Amazing! Incredible!' called Lizzie's mum, rushing onto the field.

'You're all a credit to the school,' said Miss Jones, beaming. 'The boys' team has got a lot to live up to now!'

Everyone hugged each other, including Daniel, and he didn't seem to mind. In fact, he was the first to hug Lizzie. 'How's your nose?' he asked.

'A bit squashed still!' said Lizzie. 'But then, you always said it was too big!'

'Well done!' said Helen, shaking Lizzie's hand. 'You've got a great team. We thought you'd be a walkover. We'll have to look out for you in the League.'

Lizzie beamed. Despite all their disasters, everything

had worked out brilliantly.

She hugged Daniel. 'Thanks,' she said. 'We could never have won without you. Susie Ollorenshaw would have thought you were a hero!'

'Actually, I really enjoyed it,' said Daniel, surprising even himself. 'I never knew the game would be so hard. Girls are quite good at football, aren't they?'

'Quite good!' From Daniel that was praise indeed! Lizzie thumped him playfully. She'd never felt happier. Maybe having a little brother wasn't so bad, after all. Thank goodness he'd been there when they needed him – and thank goodness she'd found that crumpled photo of Susie Ollorenshaw in Daniel's school bag!

THE MOUTH
by Nick Warburton

It's no surprise to anyone when we lose our first game of the season. Here we go again, I think, and I'm sitting in the changing room with my elbows on my knees, really shattered. Painful Evans, our captain, drops down beside me and leans his head against the wall.

'The trouble is,' he says, 'we're not organized enough.'

I tell him the trouble is we don't score goals but he ignores me.

'Have you seen your brother about that video yet?' he asks.

Painful has been nagging on about this idea for some time now. He reckons that if my brother brings his camera to a game, we can watch what we're doing and correct our faults. He says it's what all the big clubs do.

But Wimpole Wanderers is not a big club. We play Saturday mornings on the rec. We've got six or seven

141

decent players but the rest are make-weights: lads who're more keen than they are useful, or who don't care about football but get dragged along to make up the numbers. It's like some sort of circus slap-stick routine – quite entertaining, but not football.

'Well?' says Painful. 'Have you seen him?'

'Not yet, Painful. I sort of forgot . . .'

'That's what I'm saying. We're not *organized*.'

'It's not that,' I say. 'If we had one more decent player, we might score the odd goal.'

Painful gives me a pitying look.

'You reckon there's some kid with magic feet nobody's seen before, do you? And he's going to come and play for us?'

'Well . . .'

'Do me a favour.'

In my heart I think he's right. The odds against making a real discovery must be thousands to one. But you have to give it a go, don't you? I mean, what good can a video do if you haven't got the talent?

So I decide to do a bit of scouting and I get up early on Sunday morning and cycle over to the rec to have a nose around.

There's dew on the grass. There's a thick, low mist. The early birds have just had their worms and they've gone back to sleep. Not a sign of human life. I'm just about to give up and go home when I hear a thudding sound, and this figure comes swirling out of the mist, and it's chasing a football.

I hold my breath and watch it come towards me. It puts a foot on the ball, turns . . . and I see that it's a girl. And not a very big one at that. Even Wimpole Wanderers aren't that desperate, I think.

Then she puts her toe on the ball, gives it a bit of backspin and flicks it in the air. She catches it on her knee, swivels round and sends it back where it came from. Straight and absolutely true.

Before I can move, she's run off in the direction of the ice-cream kiosk, the mist swirling aside to make way for her. I catch up in time to see her driving the ball against the kiosk wall. There's a cluster of wet round marks on the wall, all close together.

This kid can play.

'What's your name?' I call out to her.

'Julie.'

'You play for a team?'

I hold my breath. Don't let her play for someone else, I think. Let me be the one to discover her.

'No.'

'But you do like football?'

'Oh yes,' she says. 'I do like football.'

'In that case,' I tell her with a smile, 'I've got some good news for you.'

'No,' she says.

I can't quite believe it. I'm offering her the chance to walk straight into Wimpole Wanderers, and she's saying no.

'Why not?'

'I just like kicking around.'

'You *can't* just kick around. That's no test.'

'It's all I want,' she says.

She picks up the ball and I can see she's about to wander off.

'You'll only know how good you are if you play against other kids,' I say quickly. 'Football is a team game and if you're not in a team you're not playing proper football.'

For a second or two she thinks really hard, and then she nods, just a little nod, and mumbles, 'Maybe I'll give it a go, then. As long as you don't go telling everyone.'

'You don't have to worry,' I say. 'Some of the other teams have girls as well.'

'It's not that,' she says as she walks away. 'I just don't like people watching, that's all.'

So Saturday comes round, and so does Julie. She's not very big, and she hasn't got much to say for herself. She wears a spotless Spurs shirt. Of course, she's not to know but the shirt is not a good move. It gets her off on the wrong foot. Painful is an Arsenal fan.

He looks Julie up and down for a second or two and I can tell he thinks I've flipped.

'Where do you play?' he asks coldly.

'The rec mostly. We've only just moved here and . . .'

I wince, and Painful rolls his eyes to the skies.

'What position?'

'Oh, I see. I don't mind. Have you got any gaps?'

Any gaps, I think. At least five. Take your pick. But Painful says, 'Not really, but as it happens our left-winger can't play today. Eddie Simms. D'you know him?'

'No.'

'He's good.'

This is not true. Simms only plays for the chance to get himself dirty and for the half-time oranges. He flings himself all over the park, especially if it's muddy, and he specializes in sliding tackles, though never anywhere near the ball. By half-time he's usually plastered from head to foot. Then he gets stuck into the oranges, sucking at them like a vampire. He just can't get enough of them. You have to watch him or he'd have the lot.

'Play on the wing,' Painful says to Julie. 'But stay wide. I don't want you coming inside and pulling our system all over the place.'

System, I think; what system is this all of a sudden? But he tosses her a shirt and the game gets under way.

As usual, we get off to a bad start. Before Julie's even had a sniff of the ball, we concede an early goal. It comes when Stringy, our keeper, throws the ball straight at the feet of their striker. I've told him in practice: he should never throw the ball out. It's these massive fancy gloves he wears. They're like dustbin lids and he has no proper control over them.

Anyway, five minutes later the ball breaks to the left – accidentally, I think – and Julie takes it to the dead-ball line and hooks back a cross which Painful meets at the near post. A thumping header: one–all.

Painful goes down like a sack of spuds. He's lying there, arms and legs spread, a kind of starfish in the mud. Even though it's his head that's been thumped, he writhes about, clutching his knee. He must be dazed: he usually knows which bit to clutch.

'I'll be all right,' he says. 'It's just a bit painful.'

Which is how he got his name. He takes a knock in most games, and they're always just a bit painful. This time, though, he really is shaken up. I give our sub a wave. He takes no notice because he's sitting on his sports bag reading the *Beano*.

'Am I imagining things,' Painful mumbles, 'or did Julie cross that ball?'

I can see it's not just the ball that's laid him out. It's confusion. He can't believe a girl can cross like that.

After that, more and more passes find their way to the left wing – only now they're deliberate – and Julie weaves down the touchline like a cat in an alley. Their defence is pulled over to cope with her. Which means lovely big gaps in the middle. I score one to take us ahead. Painful adds another. Even Mark Todd, who usually looks like someone tap-dancing underwater, manages to trickle one over the line. Then Julie herself chips over their goalie, and we run out 5–1 winners. We didn't score five goals in a single game last season.

We've never known a season like this one. It's not just that Julie plays well – though she does, needless to say – but we *all* begin to improve. And after every game, Julie picks up her stuff and off she goes. She never hangs around for a chat. We never find out where she lives. In fact, we don't even know her full name. She just turns up, dead on time, plays a blinder and disappears again.

One day a bloke from the local paper arrives to take a team photo. Most of us think this is great, and start smarming our hair down and looking cool. But Julie sits apart and she just shakes her head.

'No,' she says. 'No photo.'

And she won't budge, so they take the photo with Eddie Simms instead, and he stands there grinning like mad with his chest out and his arms folded.

Well, we reckon that's all right. It's obviously what she wants, and it suits us to have her playing, so it's all right.

Till we come to the quarter-final of the Cup. It's a pretty tight game but, thanks to a couple of goals from Julie, we win. And that is historic. No-one can re-member us reaching the semi-final before and, naturally enough, we're all hopping from foot to foot with the thrill of it all.

'The semi-final, lads!' says Painful. 'The crowds will flock!'

And the lads all cheer.

Then I notice that Julie hasn't sloped off like she usu-ally does. She's hanging around for a word with Painful.

'I was thinking,' she says quietly, 'maybe you should give Eddie Simms a bit of a run.'

'Simms?' laughs Painful. 'He's useless. The only running we get from Simms is from his nose.'

'The thing is,' she mutters, picking the mud off her boots and looking uncomfortable, 'I'm not sure I can make it.'

'Not make the semi-final? Why?'

'It's just a bit awkward.'

'But the crowds will be out. This is the Big One.'

'Well, that's just it. I'm not happy about the crowds and the publicity and stuff.'

'Believe me, Julie,' Painful says firmly, 'Wimpole Wanderers is depending on you.'

In the end she agrees, but I can tell she's not happy about it. She kind of sags her shoulders and looks as if it's a big chore. It's a real puzzle.

Anyway, Painful doesn't notice any of this. All he can think about is the semi-final, so he's just glad she's playing.

The semi-final has caused a considerable noise. Everyone's talking about it, it seems, especially Painful. He takes me to one side and puts an arm round my shoulder.

'No messing this time,' he says. 'We *have* to get that video.'

Rather than tell him I think it's a waste of time, I sigh and say OK; I'll ask my brother to do his *Match of the Day* bit.

'Only don't tell the others,' says Painful. 'They'll only stop playing to grin at the camera.'

★

So the big day comes and we're all a bit nervous. After all, there's about fifty or sixty people waiting to see us play, including my brother with his gear. Normally we only get mums and dads and a dog or two, and they don't always stay to the end.

Julie arrives looking pale and depressed, with her shoulders sagged even lower.

'It's supposed to be fun,' I tell her. 'Let's just go out and enjoy it.'

And she gives me a pathetic smile, as if I'd suggested going down to the dentist to get our teeth filled.

As it turns out, the team we're playing is quite beatable. A couple of minutes in and we're all thinking, we can do this; we can go all the way. And we begin to take a grip. Mind you, we do it without much help from Julie who keeps stopping to gawp at the crowd. I'm wondering what's got into her, when, suddenly, there's this amazing sergeant-major bellow.

'Get stuck in, Wimpole! GET STUCK IN!'

There on the touchline is a bloke in a flashy red tracksuit. His face is all creased up, like a huge angry baby, and he pounds up and down, trying to keep level with the play.

'No, no, NO, Wimpole! Pass and run! PASS AND RUN! You call that running? I've got beans that run faster than that!'

It's so grim that one or two of the other spectators drift over to the opposite side of the pitch. I try to ignore it but it begins to get to me. It begins to get

to all of us, though it's Julie who comes in for the worst of it.

'OH WHAT A NELLY! CAN'T YOU CHASE, YOU STEAMING GREAT NELLY?'

And she hangs her head and fades even further out of the game.

At half-time Painful gathers us round for a chat.

'What's got into you? You're not even trying.'

'It's the Mouth,' I say. 'The bloke in the tracksuit. He's putting us off.'

'He's a complete pilchard,' says Stringy. 'He nearly made me drop that corner. Who is he?'

Everyone is mumbling that they don't know but how they wish he'd just clear off when Julie, most unusually, chips in.

'I know him,' she sighs. 'He's my dad.'

And the penny drops. No name, no address, and definitely no photo. The poor kid has been trying to keep her football a secret all season, and the fuss about the semi-final has blown it.

Her dad's found out. He's turned up.

And it's like a giant thumb coming out of the sky to squash her flat. Because that's how she looks when she tells us: squashed.

'I didn't mean it,' Stringy says to Julie as he trots back to his goal. 'I didn't actually mean he was a pilchard.'

Julie just gives him a half smile. Then the whistle goes and we're back in the most important game of our lives. But we're on half revs: we've all got one eye on the ball

151

and the other on Julie's dad. And he makes sure we know he's there.

'Wimpole Wanderers? Don't make me laugh! Wimps, more like! COME ON! No, DON'T run with it! PASS and run! PASS, you nelly! NOT LIKE THAT, you no-good useless NERD!!'

Of course, the nelly-in-chief is Julie. And we have to admit, it's the worst game she's ever played for us.

We fail to score, but, luckily, so do they. It's a 0–0 draw and we live to fight again. Just.

Afterwards, Painful wanders over to Julie and tries to cheer her up.

'You should take no notice,' he says. 'You know you're good, don't you?'

She doesn't bother to answer.

'Look, if it makes it easier, we *could* give Eddie Simms a game . . .'

'You don't want me to play?'

'Of course I do, but . . . well, you know . . .'

'Dad knows about Wimpole Wanderers now, and he wants me to play.'

'Yes but . . .'

'Football means everything to him, Painful. And he's got this cranky knee so he can't play. *He* can't play but *I* can. So I have to, don't I? Even though I'm a nelly.'

It's a pity he hasn't got a cranky jaw, I think, because he's ruined your game. And I wonder what I can do about it.

★

A couple of days before the replay, I suggest we all meet at my house to talk over tactics. No-one is very keen. Especially Julie. Of course, I know why: she lives the other side of town, so the Mouth will have to come and pick her up afterwards. She doesn't want him anywhere near Wimpole Wanderers if she can help it. It's sad, really.

Anyway, Painful sets up these charts, all marked up with coloured pens, so he can talk us through a few things.

'How about the video?' I ask him.

'Video?' he says miserably. 'I'm not so sure now.'

'I think you'll find it interesting.'

'Maybe,' he says. 'Later.'

So we all stare at Painful's charts, though no-one really understands them. Or tries to. They all think the team's been knocked back to square one. The flair's gone.

An hour goes by and then this car draws up outside. It's a flashy job with those headlights that go up and down like a frog's eyes. And sure enough, out of it gets the Mouth.

The room goes quiet and we hear this booming voice in the hall.

'I had no idea she was in a team . . . She could be quite good, if only she'd listen to a bit of advice now and then.'

Some of the lads look at Julie, and Julie looks at the floor. I pick up the video cassette and nudge Painful with it.

'Pity to waste it,' I say.

'OK,' he says half-heartedly. 'Put it on.'

Which is exactly what I was hoping for. I close the curtains and smile at the lads. They sit there like a row of skittles. They know how they played and they're not keen to see it again.

To begin with, there's nothing but coloured shirts whizzing backwards and forwards, and you can't learn much from that. But it doesn't really matter. Tactics are not the point. The video whirrs on and I hear the door at the back open. The Mouth has come in, and he's standing there watching. I lean forward and turn up the sound.

'No, no, NO, Wimpole!' comes fog-horning out of the set. 'Pass and run! PASS AND RUN! You call that running? I've got beans that run faster than that!'

I take a quick look round at the figure by the door. He's standing there, his eyes glued to the screen, his mouth half open. But silent.

'OH WHAT A NELLY! CAN'T YOU CHASE, YOU STEAMING GREAT NELLY?'

And on and on. This flashy tracksuit jumping up and down, bawling out insults and abuse. It's embarrassing. It's acutely embarrassing.

The screen goes blank and I switch the set off and open the curtains.

When I turn round to face the room, everyone is staring at the blank screen, not daring to move. Everyone but the Mouth. He's slipped out. Julie has gone, too.

★

We turn up for the replay and suddenly there are the orange nets and the corner posts and fresh white lines on the grass, and the sight of all this makes me tingle. We're gathered around studying the pitch, as if somehow it's going to tell us the secret of the game. No-one says very much, but Painful sidles up to me for a quiet word.

'Any sign?'

That's all he says but I know what he means. No-one's seen anything of Julie since that day in my house. He's worried about the game. So am I, but I'm worried about Julie, too. I don't know how she took all that video stuff. I'm the one who found her, I think, and maybe now I'm the one who lost her, and it's not a thought that makes me happy.

'No sign,' I say.

Painful sighs and nods at Simms who turns instantly white and drags his tracksuit off. A minute before the whistle I'm flat out on the ground, warming up with a few press-ups, when these feet appear in front of my eyes. Small feet in small boots. I look up and, yes, it's Julie. She's staring down at me. And she's smiling.

'You're here,' I say, hauling myself up.

'Of course I'm here,' she says.

'She's here!' I call to the others.

'She's here!' yells Simms, and climbs back into his tracksuit with this fantastic look of relief all over his face. I've never seen him move so fast.

155

Then I see the Mouth standing on the touchline. Oh no, I think. Back to square one. But it isn't. There's something different about him. He catches my eye and gives a little nod. A *quiet* little nod. And he's wearing a sensible jacket and grey trousers. Sober, I suppose you'd call them. Yes, he's very different.

So the game gets under way, and it's pretty tense stuff. I mean, anyone would get worked up just watching. A *fish* would get worked up at that match. But when I glance over at the Mouth, he's clapping. Clapping politely, with his mouth firmly shut. And that's how he stays throughout the match. You'd hardly know he was there.

And we win, of course; mostly because Julie plays a blinder. An absolute blinder. The best we've ever seen. It's enough to make anyone want to cheer.

GO! GO! CHICHICO!
by Geraldine McCaughrean

He was first down on the beach that morning. A few seagulls were pecking at the litter along the water-line, but no-one else was about. The sun was still so low that it bobbed like a big football on the sea. Chichico wanted to swim out and fetch it; then he would not have to wait for the others. Chichico was always first to arrive on the beach, but he could not start playing till Anna and Esidio arrived with the ball.

They used their T-shirts for goal posts, and Anna and Esidio both played against Chichico, because he was so good. As the morning wore on, more and more children arrived and joined in.

Some rich boys staying in the big hotels along the back of the beach sometimes wanted to play. If she liked the look of them, Anna would point at their expensive

157

trainers and say, 'Shoes off! Shoes off! No-one here wears shoes!'

So the boys joined in, barefoot, and Chichico ran them ragged, while his friends chanted, 'Go! Go! Chichico!'

The truth was, none of the local boys so much as owned a pair of shoes between them. But what did they care? The sand was soft.

That morning, up at one of the hotel windows, two men stood watching the game on the beach below.

'Look how he wrong-foots them. Every time! Look at the speed of him!' said one.

'And you see how he controls the ball?' said the other. 'Shall I go down and have a word?'

'Do that, will you? And don't take no for an answer.'

Chichico saw a man beckon him from the steps of the hotel. He tried to take no notice. Strangers in suits rarely had anything good to say to a barefoot boy. Last month a football had broken one of the hotel windows. This was probably the manager wanting to move the game on down the beach. But the man went on beckoning, and at last Chichico hopped and sidled over to within earshot.

'You ever heard of Santos?' said the man in the suit.

'Santos who? I had an uncle once . . .'

'The football team, boy. Santos Brazil.'

'I'd have to be dead not to,' said Chichico coolly. 'They're only the greatest side in the entire universe.'

'Well the Santos scout has been watching you. Why

not come along for a trial on Friday? We might be able to make a real footballer of you. What's your name?'

Just for a moment, Chichico could not remember. He could not remember his name, nor how to breathe nor even how to speak. 'Chi-chi-chi,' he stammered.

'OK, Chi Chi. Be at the stadium on Friday, early. And remember to bring your boots.'

Chichico sat down on the hotel steps. They seemed to tip and roll under him like a raft at sea. Anna and Esidio came running over.

'Are we playing football or what?' said Esidio.

'Tell me I'm awake. Tell me I'm not dreaming,' whispered Chichico.

'Don't think so,' said Esidio, pinching himself.

'I've got a trial for Santos,' whispered Chichico. 'On Friday.'

Esidio pinched himself again. 'On second thoughts, I think you are dreaming. But tell you what . . . don't let's wake up till Saturday!'

The only problem was the boots. Chichico murmured in a daze that he needed boots, must have boots. Esidio waved a hand breezily in the air. 'Don't give it a thought!' he said grandly. 'I'll buy you a pair. You can pay me back when you're a famous football star!'

'You're the best, 'Sid,' said Chichico, and went speeding away to tell his mother, his bare heels throwing up the sand in spurts of golden dust.

'And just how are you going to buy a pair of football boots?' said Anna to her brother. 'Have you any idea how much they cost?'

'I'll think of something,' said Esidio, refusing to let his sister spoil the happy mood. 'Just so long as he plays in those trials. That's what matters.'

On Friday, Anna went with Chichico to the huge white stadium on the hill. It was part of their lives – the palace in every Brazilian child's personal fairy tale. Dozens of other young hopefuls were standing about, knock-kneed with terror, just like Chichico. Esidio was late getting there.

'He's not coming, is he? He won't come with the boots, will he? He can't face telling me, can he?'

Anna shrugged helplessly. 'He'll be here,' she said loyally. And suddenly, there he was.

'Did you get them? Did you? You didn't, did you?' Chichico greeted him.

'Don't work up a sweat before you have to!' said his mate, swaggering about, playing the clown, as he magically produced from behind his back a superb shining pair of black boots. They had chevrons of yellow, and laces that shone like cords of liquorice.

'They're only the best money can buy, that's all!' declared Esidio.

Before Chichico had time to thank him, a steward pinned a number to the back of his vest and barked at him to 'get out on the pitch with the rest'. Chichico could not have found the words, anyway.

'All right. Own up. Where did you get them?' said

161

Anna, icily. 'What did you sell? Our mother?'

'I just *borrowed* them. From one of the lockers in the changing rooms. They've probably played in Cup finals, those boots!' He tried to sound proud of himself, but Esidio had never stolen anything before, not in his whole life, and his sister could see he was scared right down to the soles of his bare feet.

'If you borrow something, you ought to ask permission,' she said warily.

'There wasn't anyone . . .'

'So write a note.'

Esidio was startled. 'A confession, you mean?'

Anna rocked her head from side to side. 'More of an I.O.U. – saying you only borrowed them – it was an emergency, say.'

'I can't spell emergency,' murmured Esidio, failing to mention all the other words she knew he could not spell.

'I'll write it for you,' said Anna, encouragingly hooking her arm through his. 'We don't even have to put your name on it. We'll slip it under the locker room doors. They'll understand. And after the trials I'll come with you when you give them back. You can't get arrested for borrowing something. I'm sure, almost.'

Esidio looked grateful. 'I thought you'd be angry. Mum would be. Mum would say I was a thieving sinner past all hope of Heaven.'

'I wasn't suggesting we tell Mum,' said Anna. 'Just so

long as Chichico plays in these trials, eh? One worry at a time.'

But it was strange playing in boots. When Chichico set off to run, his feet felt like lead. He reached the ball, but the smallest kick skyed it over the touchline in among the empty seats.

'You're rubbish,' said a boy in snow-white boots, hacking at Chichico's shin.

And his legs got so tired! He clumped about the field like a girl wearing her mother's high heels. Before long, he was too slow even to catch up with the run of play. The ball came flying past him one last time, and he turned to play it. But the unfamiliar studs gripped the turf, and Chichico only fell over, twisting his knee.

'Who invited you along?' jeered the boy in white boots.

A whistle blew. 'Take a break!' called the coach. 'Numbers twelve, thirty-six, seven and twenty can go home. We don't need you.'

Chichico hardly needed to check the number on his shirt. But there it was. Twenty. He had just thrown away the chance of a lifetime.

He looked around him at the concrete stands gleaming in the sun. Only once in his life had he ever had a ticket to watch Santos play here. He remembered every minute – the flags, the drums, the whistles, the huge roar as Santos scored. Now the stadium looked like a vast white liner on the point of setting sail without him.

163

'. . . let you go,' he thought, blinking back his tears.
'. . . t. I can't.'

He had to be rid of them. Inside the stadium, everyone's eyes were on the trials. It was easy for Chichico to creep into the dark building and hide his football boots.

He apologized to the boots. Inwardly he apologized to Esidio for all the trouble he had gone to. But I can't play in boots. Of course I can't. I've *never* played in boots! he thought, as he stuffed them to the dark rear of a tin cupboard. From by the door came a noise – the tiniest scraping sound, so that Chichico froze in terror. Someone was about to come in. They would ask him what he was doing there: he would have to explain . . .

But the person at the door did not come in. A light pair of feet – maybe two pairs – sprinted softly away down the long concrete corridor. Chichico waited five minutes, then his bare feet did the same. At the end of the tunnel, he bumped into Anna and Esidio. They looked even worse than he had felt five minutes ago. But then they had had to watch while Chichico let his big chance slip away from him for ever.

'What happened out there?' said Anna sympathetically. 'Were you nervous? Was that it?'

Chichico grinned. 'No! It was the boots! I can't play in boots! But it'll be all right now. They've gone. I've got rid of them. Next time I'll play barefoot – and then see! Can't stop now!' He leapt off along the terraces, as agile as a mountain goat on his bare brown feet.

Esidio's groan came from the bottom of his soul. 'So he's got rid of the boots. Now I can't put them back. And I just admitted to taking them! I'll go to prison, probably. I'll go to Hell for stealing, that's definite. I wouldn't have minded . . . really – if Chichico had just got to play for Santos!'

Then Esidio put his face in his hands and wept.

Anna rested her hand on his hair. 'Don't worry. I'll come to prison with you. If they let girls in.'

The coach, too, gave a deep and heartfelt groan. 'No,' he was saying to himself. 'Nothing here. Not one spark of real talent.'

'Excuse me, Sir,' said Chichico.

'Don't bother me, boy. You're number twenty, aren't you? No second chances. Go home. We can't use you.'

'Please, Sir. I can't go home.'

'Scram, I said.'

'I can't go home, because *somebody has stolen my boots*, and if I go home without them my cruel father will beat me and my saintly mother will break her poor heart and then what will become of my fifteen little brothers and sisters?'

The coach blinked at this outburst. 'Boots? I can't worry about boots now,' he said vaguely. 'Hang about till the trials are over and I'll send for the police.'

'Yes, Sir. Thank you, Sir,' said Chichico meekly, and perched on a bench. After a moment he coughed and said, 'Maybe I could just go and kick the ball about, while I wait.'

'What, in your bare feet?'

'Why not?' said Chichico. And before anyone could say no, he had run onto the pitch.

He took the ball from the boy in white boots and snaked round two other players. He passed quickly to the wing, and as the ball was crossed back to him, headed it firmly into the top corner of the net.

In the manager's box, the coach got to his feet.

After that, the other side hardly touched the ball. It spun between their knees, looped over their heads, it disappeared from the very toes of their boots, as Chichico smacked it goalwards.

In his dugout, the coach stood on his seat to get a better view.

The boy in white boots tried to stamp on Chichico's bare toes, but was spotted by the referee and sent off. Before he reached the stand, Chichico had scored another goal.

The coach jumped up and down so hard that his seat broke. '*Sign that boy! Sign that barefoot boy!*'

'Now I can go to prison happy!' declared Esidio. 'I think I'll go and own up to what I did.'

'I'll go with you!' said Anna staunchly.

The Santos first team were in the changing room, putting on their practice kit. Esidio and Anna hovered nervously in the doorway, waiting for the robbery to be discovered. Great beads of sweat stood out on Esidio's forehead. Anna saw them as she took a long hard look at her beloved brother: the one she had just consigned to prison with her stupid advice. Write a note, indeed! What had possessed her to suggest . . .

Then she saw it. A midfielder's big bare foot was standing squarely on top of the note they had pushed under the changing-room door. He had not seen it yet. No-one had seen it. Now if Anna could just retrieve it.

'You kids shouldn't be in here,' he said, noticing Esidio and Anna lurking in the doorway.

'No . . . I suppose . . . Er . . . We . . . I mean . . .'

'We just wanted your autograph,' said Anna, advancing a few steps into the room.

'Do you make a habit of going into men's changing rooms, little girl?' said the midfielder sourly, and was just about to push her forcibly outside when he noticed the note under his foot. 'What's this?'

From the other end of the room came the booming moose-call of a man speaking with his head inside a tin locker. 'Eh! Enrico! What are your boots doing in my locker?' shouted the Santos goalkeeper.

'Search me,' said the centre half, and took the black boots – the beautiful, shining boots with their chevron of yellow and their laces like liquorice – and began lacing them on. Esidio and Anna stared open-mouthed. So *that* was where Chichico had 'got rid' of them!

The midfielder unfolded the note and had just begun to read when Anna snatched it out of his hand with a 'That's mine!' and darted for the door, dragging her brother after her. Her voice echoed back along the long concrete corridor. '. . . Just a fan letter, mister . . . !'

Outside, in the sunlight, Esidio tugged free and leaned against a wall to catch his breath, panting and laughing and coughing all at once. 'Do me a favour, Anna,' he said.

'What's that, 'Sid?'

'Don't let's tell Chichico about any of this. It might spoil his concentration.'

'Do me a favour, 'Sid,' said Anna in reply.

'What's that, Anna?'

'Don't let's tell Mum *any* of this. Ever.'

The newspapers were full of it. Chichico was the youngest Brazilian ever to play in the first team. And of course he was the first ever to play barefoot in a Cup Final!

On the day of the match, his parents, his brothers and all his friends from the beach had tickets bought with his very own wages. They were up there now in the stands, waving flags, blowing whistles and singing. But mostly they were chanting, 'Go! Go! Chichico! Go! Go! Chichico!'

Anna nudged Esidio during the half-time break and said, 'He looks so tiny beside all those great big men.' But Esidio called her silly, and said that it did not take size or muscles to be a great footballer. Esidio often said this. He was only knee-high to a grasshopper himself.

In the second half, Chichico pelted up and down the field, tackling, passing, heading the ball across the goal-mouth and shadowing a player twice his size. It was an even, desperate match. The crowd were swaying with emotion: they even fell quiet towards the end, which was almost unheard-of.

It was then that Chichico heard a Santos player shout his name. He saw the ball at his feet and the open goal-mouth ahead of him. He did not have time to shift his weight. Instinctively he hit the ball.

There was a thunderclap as every seat in the stadium folded shut and the entire crowd leaped to their feet. Then the roar built up until it seemed to shake the oval sky. 'A goal! A goal! Chichico has scored!'

FOOTBALL FEVER 2

Tony Bradman

*Goals galore and plenty of action – from kick-off
to the final whistle!*

Meet Craig, who takes advice from a phantom footballer
to help his team on a goal-scoring run in the league
championship; Dave, an inexperienced goalie, who must
make split-second decisions in a penalty shoot-out; Olly, a
top striker who devises some new team tactics just before
the semi-finals of the cup; and a whole squad of other
talented young players – goalies, defenders, midfielders and
strikers.

Celebrate the goals, applaud the great saves and hold your
breath for those edge-of-the-seat matchplay moments in
this new collection of brand new, never-before-published
soccer stories from a team of top authors including Rob
Childs, Narinder Dhami and Paul Stewart.

ISBN 0-552-54527-9

A CORGI ORIGINAL PAPERBACK